12.–

Arctic Summer

Arctic Summer

E.M. Forster

100 PAGES
Published by Hesperus Press Limited
4 Rickett Street, London SW6 1RU
www.hesperuspress.com

First published in 1980 in *Arctic Summer and Other Fiction*
First published by Hesperus Press Limited, 2003

ISBN: 1-84391-061-6

CONTENTS

FOREWORD

One cannot help feeling somewhat guilty on reading *Arctic Summer*; it is so like stepping behind the curtains drawn across a stage and catching the actors rehearsing for a play, or opening a door and coming upon preparations for a party, or a surprise. One feels one would like to ask E.M. Forster's permission to read what he clearly considered unfinished, an experiment he abandoned.

That is also, precisely, its fascination. One can actually follow the work as it progressed – or did not – and the doubts and worries of a scrupulous mind agonising over the knotty technical details as well as the moral value of the theme as he pursued it – 'the antithesis,' he said, 'between the civilised man, who hopes for an Arctic Summer, and the heroic man who rides into the sea'.

Forster had been holidaying in Italy in the summer of 1911, and on 27th September that year jotted down an entry in his diary: 'idea for a book on chivalry'. That was precisely the moment when Italy declared war on Turkey over Tripoli. Forster, sympathetic to Turkey, wrote some scenes for a novel in what is now called the 'Tripoli Fragment', voicing his uneasiness that 'Italy has blotted her shield'. These fragments contain the seeds of what, in November, he began to call 'Arctic Summer'.

Of course no single idea ever leads to the writing of a novel (unlike a poem or a short story); it is invariably a confluence of ideas – some visible, some unconscious – that creates sufficient fire and energy for a sustained piece of writing.

Some of these can be quite trivial. On 24th September Forster wrote a letter to Josie Darling describing the return journey from Italy and the pandemonium at Basle station:

'hundreds of tourists struggling for half that number of seats on the midnight train, and shouting that all would be well if the others would behave like Gentlemen'.

This was to be the opening scene of the novel, and in November Forster made diary entries that revealed some of the ideas that fed into it. One records a discussion with Roger Fry over the necessity of excluding sentiment in the form of 'reminiscences' and 'Romanticism' from aesthetic form, a discussion that he ascribed in the novel to Martin Whitby and his wife, Venetia, over a fresco they see in the sixteenth-century castle Tramonta (said to be based on Malpaga, near Bergamo) that depicts an earlier war between Christians and Turks. Martin is struck by the resemblance of one of the figures to his new young acquaintance, Clesant March, and is gratified to learn that it is indeed a representation of one of his ancestors; Venetia, on the other hand, pooh-poohs such sentiment about 'eminent ancestors'.

In November, too, Forster wrote to Rupert Brooke to confess he had decided 'to put all I can remember of your paper on art into a novel', the paper being one that Brooke had read to the Cambridge Fabians, demanding 'Graduation of the Income Tax' and a 'State Subsidy of Literature' – demands that Forster ascribes to Martin Whitby (to whom he also gave the Quaker upbringing of Roger Fry). And Brooke, the golden-headed boy of Cambridge who went to war and died, surely contributed to the figures of Clesant and Lance March as well.

What a delicious tangle for the peeping Tom in us to delve into and untangle!

Yet by early 1912, after that initial combustion of ideas, the novel seems to have petered out. In May he noted in his diary: 'My novel awful'. He did begin a revision, opening the novel at a school called Radipole which gives its name to an alternate version, but he soon put it aside and left for India.

This now seems a providential moment in Forster's writing life. It is not that he abandoned the faltering *Arctic Summer* and so freed himself to write his masterpiece, *A Passage to India*, but, in continuing to play with those initial ideas that were somehow not coming right, he was able to channel them into a magnificently wider, deeper river.

While in India, he read the *Bhagavadgītā*, that dialogue between Lord Krishna and the warrior Arjuna on the eve of the great battle described in the epic *Mahabharata*, and in February 1913 he wrote to Forrest Reid from the city of Allahabad that 'the only book I have in my head is too like *Howards End* to interest me: a contrast again: between battle and work: the chief figure a Knight errant born too late in time who finds no clear issue to which to devote himself: our age demands patient good-tempered labour, not chivalry.' He went on to claim: 'I want something beyond the field of action and behaviour: the waters of the river that rises from the middle of the earth to join the Ganges and the Jumna where they join' (a reference to the mythical river Saraswati that is said to be the invisible one in a confluence of three in the city of Allahabad that makes it a place of pilgrimage for Hindus).

Perhaps it was the difficulty of fitting what he saw as an anachronistic theme onto the modern age that made him give up on *Arctic Summer*. Instead, on that Indian visit, he discovered the setting in which he could fully and expansively explore the importance of the heroic act, performed in *A Passage to India* by Adela Quested and Fielding, who go against the rigidly regulated system of a colonial society and break through to another – and are saved.

Yet Forster never gave up on *Arctic Summer* either. In June 1951, when he read it at the Aldeburgh Festival, he revised the first five chapters, turning it into the text we now have, the first half of which sets out the 'antithesis' that provides the necessary tension, and the second half exploring the directions into which such opposing beliefs and natures may lead.

By combining aspects of himself, Roger Fry and Rupert Brooke in Martin Whitby, Forster created a hero for the troubled, ambivalent world in which he himself lived. Martin announced: 'my era is to have no dawn. It is to be a kind of Arctic Summer, in which there will be time to get something really great done. Dawn implies twilight and we have decided to abolish them both.' But this 'hero' is also the coward who flees from a burning cinema hall, abandoning his companion, then is overcome with horror and shame, only to have his cool, sensible wife inform him: 'Aristide got out as safely without you as he would have with you.' She also points out: 'It's merely your reflex action, working slower than most people's... in ninety-nine cases out of a hundred, ten seconds is *not* too late. In all the important affairs of life there is this ten seconds' interval for deciding.'

So much for the cool, rational, modern way of thinking. The wild, romantic, chivalric one is personified by the brothers March. There is a scene in which the two young men spend a day out riding in the country around their gloomy Northumbrian estate, and come upon a hunt in which they enthusiastically participate. '"I'm glad we happened on that,"' Clesant says. '"I hate wasting a morning."' In the glow of that glorious incident – prey torn to bits, a child ritually bloodied – Lance becomes more ruminative and asks his brother, '"Do you go falling in love, Cles?"' Clesant chaffs him for this, only to find that his brother is in no mood for it. '"You've not understood… I don't mean anything decent. It's getting a damned nuisance."' Clesant responds by feeling 'miserably unhappy. He changed the subject,' but he has to face up to the facts when a telegram arrives from Cambridge, informing him that Lance is being sent down and imploring his brother to 'stick to' him. Clesant does not; he denounces his brother so violently that Lance takes the kind of drastic action that the code of chivalry demands. Sex and death: their explosive coming together appears to have stopped Forster short.

The events are rushed and packed into nine short chapters, a mere eighty-two pages. Had there been more room, we should surely have had fuller, richer portraits of, say, Venetia the cool and scholarly, her livelier, more original sister Dorothea, who 'made up for the thousands of young ladies who have pretended not to fall in love until they are loved', their father, Sir Hugh Borlase, the master of Lance's college in Cambridge, who is called a 'pantaloon' and a 'pulchinello' but never appears on the scene, the March brothers' Uncle Vullamy, and others. Instead, Forster rushed on with the events as if he were compelled to put them down before they dissipated and vanished.

The rush and hurry charge the language with an extra liveliness and energy; of course, Forster was incapable of writing a dull or lifeless line. And we are fortunate to have the books we have. In this case, we have one as filled with ideas, suggestions and implications as a pod is with seeds that can be stored, and sowed, elsewhere.

– *Anita Desai, 2003*

NOTE ON THE TEXT

Forster began work on what was to become *Arctic Summer* in 1911, but, despite numerous drafts, he never completed it to his satisfaction. He appears to have abandoned the project in 1912, returning to it only in 1951 when he revised the first five chapters for a reading at the Aldeburgh Festival that June. The remainder of the work he neither revised nor read at the Festival; he instead delivered a 'Note' saying 'that's all I want to read, because now it goes off, at least I think so, and I do not want my voice to go out into the air while my heart is sinking.' He went on to outline several 'problems' with the plot as he saw it.

Manuscripts of *Arctic Summer* therefore exist in various stages of completion and revision. Elizabeth Ellem, Archivist at King's College at the time of Forster's death and responsible for cataloguing and preserving his papers, identified four distinguishable drafts, namely the 'Cyril', 'Tramonta', 'Radipole' and 'Aldeburgh' versions. When the work was first published, in *Arctic Summer and Other Fiction* (The Abinger Edition: London, Edward Arnold, 1980), the editor, Elizabeth Heine, grouped together these last three as the 'Main Version', and included various editorial annotations to enable both the original version and Forster's Aldeburgh revisions to be identified. Also included in the Abinger volume are the 'Tripoli Fragment', the 'Radipole Version', and various supplementary material listing further editorial changes.

The text reproduced here is that of Heine's 'Main Version' but with all Forster's 1951 revisions carried out and incorporated. Slight inaccuracies that Forster himself did not correct have been preserved.

Arctic Summer

CHAPTER ONE

'Gentlemen! Gentlemen!' Basle station echoed to the cry. 'If only other people would behave like gentlemen.' It was early on an August morning, and the passengers from the Boulogne train, mostly English, were trying to decant themselves into the train for Lucerne and the south. Difficult, for the Lucerne train was smaller, and they were beginning to fight. They did not want to fight, but by Jingo they could not avoid it; there was nothing else to do. Without losing their tempers, they scrummed and wedged and hit one another behind the knee with suitcases, and snatched at the brass bars of the train as it backed itself to a standstill. Some had ladies with them, and claimed prior treatment on that account. 'Steady on, sir, you might consider the ladies.' Others cried, 'Bother the ladies.' One tourist was pushed beneath the incoming wheels, another rescued him, and still the appeal for gentlemanliness arose, that password into a city whose gates are barred for ever.

The station, immense and modern, paid no heed. Not even the daily transit of the Island Race was an event to her, the changing-house of Europe. Trains ran into her from four or five countries, washed and shaved themselves, ate in her refreshment rooms, and rebooked when necessary; she thought in terms of trains. Behind her lay a town on a swift green river, but she only served the town as an afterthought. Its needs were little to her, its memories of a Medieval Council nothing; she was indifferent to Cardinals and Kings, and to all but efficiency.

Now the tourist Martin Whitby had spied the Lucerne train reposing at a distant platform, had measured it with his eye, had calculated where the end of the carriage would be when it drew up. Telling Venetia (his wife) and Lady Borlase (his mother-in-law) to keep out of the crowd, he had slipped past the others, and laid a gloved hand on the door. The rush followed. He was swept sideways by the train and off his legs by the crowd, and it was he who was nearly killed. The man who saved him had the look and gesture of a warrior. He impressed Martin very much, and when the train had started he set out down the corridor to find him and to thank him.

There was plenty of room after all. Everyone had found a seat and nearly everyone had forgotten the fight. A few ladies were still saying, 'I never saw such a scene in my life', but the gentlemen had lit up their pipes and were showing maps to one another. They were all alike, as Englishmen are apt to be in Switzerland – healthy chaps, rather common – and Martin could not be sure which of them had saved him from death. He tried once, and was involved in a long explanation. 'Oughtn't to get into a train when it's moving – dangerous thing to do,' was the reply. Strangers always patronized Martin. Presently he found the warrior; a disappointment; he had shrunk into a fair-haired ordinary public-school type: very clean. Martin put him down as a Wykehamite[1].

'Excuse me, sir,' said Martin, lifting his hat; 'I think you saved me from going under the train. I am very grateful to you.'

'Oh, was it you?' said the other, awkwardly; he was with friends, and they all seemed offended.

'Yes, me,' replied Martin. He stood smiling in the doorway for a moment, then lifted his hat again and went away. He had hoped that the man would prove immense, but bore the disappointment philosophically. No doubt, when death is sucking one's feet into her mouth, any human being seems immense, and gesture that saves, heroic. But the man had merely done for him what he would have hoped to do for anyone else; and it was nonsense to elevate him into a hero; unfair besides.

The train was steaming through industrial Switzerland. Martin looked tolerantly at the scene, admiring it where possible, leaving it without regret. The morning was grey, the hills very green, with battalions of larch and pine advancing between them. In the valleys lay villages and little towns busy making useful articles and joined by greasy white roads. It was a bastard country, forgotten as soon as seen, and grievous to the aesthetic eye. But our tourist had long since taken himself in hand. He knew that much of the earth must be dull and commercial, and that to revolt against her is ridiculous. Until she changed, his own thoughts contented him.

These were chiefly about his work. He was a clerk in the Treasury, and had had a very hard time of it since the beginning of the year. Night after night he had stopped late, or had taken masses of papers back to their little flat. Fagged out, he had come perilously near the state in which a holiday ceases to be attractive. Would everything go right in his absence? Would his little place be adequately filled? Would his own particular sum be totted up correctly? In the night train, he had thought of the Treasury exclusively, and it had whirled him not towards Switzerland or through France, but away from certain files in a room in Whitehall. His head had remained in communication with those files: it telephoned to them all night, and they replied, 'We cannot do without you; we are being misunderstood: we, the country, the Empire, will be ruined, all on account of your holiday.' But morning had eased the nightmare. Then he had slipped under the train and actually felt the better for it: the shock had pulled him together, and though he still thought of his work, it was benignly.

He also thought of his infant, Hugo, aged three. Then he thought of Venetia – not acutely; few of his thoughts were acute, but again with benignity and with gratitude and affection. She too was leaving her work: their eyes had met in the darkened cottage, and he had felt her a comrade as well as a wife. To Lady Borlase he also devoted a moment – kind hostile Lady Borlase – and then returned to the scenery. Though the weather was bad and the hills ignoble, he knew that he was in Switzerland: that the hills would grow immense presently and be pierced by a little black hole, through which would be Italy, and perhaps the sun.

A hand slipped into his coat pocket.

'I was wanting that book of Jaurès[2],' said his wife. 'I wanted to show mother something in it, but what's the good, what's the good?'

'Have you been arguing with her?'

'She has been so absurd. Because Switzerland can't have a navy and never has had a king, she pretends it is decadent.'

'It may be decadent, but it is the future.'

'Well, do come and put that to mother. You remember that cyclists' corps that we passed. That upset her, because it wasn't sufficiently military, and she is bringing out all father's dreary old arguments.'

'I take it that she is feeling rested.'

Venetia withdrew her hand from his coat, observing, 'How have you got so dusty?'

'I fell getting into the train – fell under it as a matter of fact, and it nearly ironed me out!'

Venetia made no comment. The might-have-been never disturbed her. She did not see herself as a widow, for she never saw herself other than as she was. Her husband continued:

'It confirms me in my dislike of corridor carriages. That man Austinson who directs the Nottingham and Derby Railway[3] – I met him the other day, and I am glad to say he agrees with me. They are going to build no more corridors, but provide each carriage with a large fold-up table, and have a really efficient lunch-basket service at the termini.'

'But they run no night expresses, the Nottingham and Derby. The arrangement would be impossible for a company that did.'

'Ah, there is that.'

Husband and wife lifted their eyes to the hills, and tried to construct the perfect train. It must be constructed – not even Basle station receives it yet – and they bent their brains on it willingly. When alone, Martin was still a little prone to dream or to mock, but in Venetia's company he always assailed some practical problem. They discussed it quietly, and not until they were returning to Lady Borlase did Venetia say, 'Don't mention your tumble to mother, she gets so nervous,' and he reply, 'Of course not.'

'Well, young people, have you found the book?' asked Lady Borlase. 'Rubbishy, rubbishy young people.'

'Yes, we have,' said Martin, whose manner had changed into a pleasing impudence. 'Meanwhile – are those sandwiches?'

'Why didn't you eat a proper breakfast at Basle?' He sat down beside her, and she peeled an apple for him, and spread a napkin over his knees, all the time grumbling gently. She was a large languid woman, but very clever, very good-hearted. To Martin she was devoted, and knew well enough that he had scamped his breakfast at Basle to get her a corner seat. After the apple she made him swallow a little sherry. Venetia took no part in these proceedings. She had no use for coaxing, deeming it a waste of the world's energy; her husband knew the food was there, and he could eat it if he liked.

'I thought you were in the restaurant-car, Martin, when you never came back to us.'

'No. None's attached. We stop for lunch at Göschenen. I was in the corridor, and afterwards talking to Venetia. I gather you did not convince her.'

'Convince Nettie! What has your generation to do with being convinced? You go in for development and many-sidedness and what is that last craze? Oh yes, rhythm. No one is convinced unless he is an old codger. Nettie would spurn the sensation.'

'That's all very well,' said Venetia, raising her eyes from Jaurès and frowning and smiling at the same time, according to her habit. 'But it doesn't prove your point against the Swiss Army, mother.'

Lady Borlase had no particular point to make, and she did honestly think her daughter too silly to be argued with. 'Let them stop indoors and do their dumb-bells,' was the best that occurred to her. She added: 'No doubt all Europe will be like them in the long run, yes, and England too. We shall all be set to do dumb-bells for half an hour every morning with an army of officials to watch us and a central bureau for appeals, and George Lloyd[4] will happen to own the only dumb-bell mine in Wales. So very curious, these coincidences. But you would call them the dawn of your new era, no doubt.'

'I should not,' replied Martin, 'for the very good reason that my new era is to have no dawn. It is to be a kind of Arctic Summer, in which there will be time to get something really great done.' (Venetia murmured, 'Arctic Summer.') 'Dawn implies twilight, and we have decided to abolish them both. Several societies exist for the purpose, to none of which you have as yet subscribed.'

'"Get something really great done",' she scoffed. 'That is so like the modern reformer. Pretentious, vague.'

'You know well enough what I want to get done. If the State would only only put aside half a million –'

'You promised the infant you wouldn't,' interposed Venetia, again smiling. 'I overheard you.' She turned to her mother. 'Dorothea and I were packing, and Martin was with Hugo in the other room. Martin said to Hugo, "Promise to be a happy boy while I am in Italy." Hugo said he would try and then said, "Father, will you be a happy boy too?" Martin said, "I will. I will never once talk to grandmamma about a State Subsidy for Literature and Art." Hugo did not understand of course, but he caught the word "subsidy", which I do think clever of him, only he got it into "tubsidy".'

'The domestic anecdote at last!' cried Martin. 'I feared it was never coming. The genuine formless pointless jointless anecdote. The mother and the woman have proved too strong for the suffragette!'

And they chattered on in the strain that pleased all three, maintaining their opinions with sincerity and yet without inconvenience, brandishing as it were the little knives that had been given to each man to defend his soul, but never proving their metal. An outsider would have thought that they were quarrelling, an intelligent foreigner that they were making conversation. Both would have been wrong.

By Göschenen the train was nearly empty. August: few of the tourists were going south of the Alps. Lucerne, looking far from lovely, had claimed most of them, and others had been dropped on the shores of the lakes, and up the valley of the Reuss. Only a handful of those who fought at Basle survived. The waiters bunched them together at one refreshment table, to make service easier, and slammed down the plates of soup.

For a time there was silence. Then Martin, lifting his head, found himself next to his rescuer, who had not got out at any of the resorts for which he was obviously destined, and who was now alone.

The following conversation took place; Martin enjoyed talking, and could always suit his remarks to his company. In this case he was neither practical nor impudent, but said:

'More room now, isn't there.'

'I beg your pardon? Oh yes, more room now.'

'Did you come straight out from England, may I ask, like ourselves?'

'No, I've been climbing, but it's been a rotten summer, a shocking summer.'

'Yes, it has been a bad summer for climbing.'

'I gave it up. There seemed no chance of the mountains clearing, so I thought I'd see Milan.'

'Very wise of you,' said Martin. 'It's just a great modern city, but well worth a visit.'

'The Cathedral's said to be fine.'

Martin agreed. Feeling sure of his ground, he added, 'You must mind to see the Galleria Vittorio Emanuele too – it's near the Cathedral; one does them together.'

'Is that where the pictures are?'

'No. They are mostly in the Brera. The Galleria is an arcade with shops and restaurants, like the Burlington Arcade – you know – but much bigger.'

Silence.

When the fish was over the stranger said, 'Do you know the country round Milan too?'

'Well, there's the Certosa. The other expeditions you might leave. Milan's more what I call a place to see than to stop in. Two or three days are plenty.'

'You don't know Tramonta[5]?'

'Tramonta?' said Martin, rather surprised. 'No, I don't. Is it near Milan?'

'There are some old paintings there.'

'Oh, very likely. There are so many paintings in Italy. But it isn't one of the usual expeditions. – You weren't thinking of the Castle in Milan itself, by any chance? There is a ceiling that they put down to Leonardo, a very well-known chap.'

'No, the paintings I mean are done by Pietro Modenese[6].'

'Hullo, you know all about it –!' Then he stopped. Know all about it? Why, the man hadn't known the Galleria from the Brera. He was crudely ignorant of Italy, and yet had heard of an obscure Cinquecentist. Turning to his mother-in-law he said, 'Lady Borlase! I say! Do you know anything about a place called Tramonta? This gentleman has been asking me.'

'I do, indeed – Can I be of any help to you? It is a charming place.'

The youth thanked her, and asked whether it was difficult to reach.

'You could probably get there in an hour in some convenient electric tram. I went in the old days, on a driving tour with my husband. You know of course what Tramonta is – a very small, very perfect, Renaissance Castle. You might pass it without seeing it, for cottages belonging to the estate have been built round it in a square, and hide it from the road. There is a moat, a drawbridge, a tiny courtyard, a tower with a wonderful view of the Alps: the Alps are not far off. It's lovely.'

'These pictures are hanging in one of the rooms, I suppose.'

'The frescoes may disappoint you. We enjoyed them, because they harmonized so well with the architecture, and because we enjoy anything that is out of date and unfashionable. – But you, Martin, would call them weak.'

'Where do they hang?' he persisted.

'Frescoes, not oils,' corrected Venetia, but the reproof conveyed nothing. Lady Borlase replied that if he would come to her carriage afterwards, she would look in her old notebook and tell him everything she remembered. 'We too are going to Italy in the hope of a little sunshine.' Then the meat course was served, and they all ate hurriedly, their eyes on the clock. The train steamed outside with a note of expectation, and the mouth of the tunnel steamed in its face. Hurrying on board they closed the windows, and the ugly grey air turned to darkness.

They emerged, but the air was still grey and ugly. It had not been a transit into the Italy of sunshine. Only the shapes of the mountains had altered, as if a soothing hand had been laid on the earth. The tortured strata sank to peace, the vegetation, the waterfalls, the buildings – all began to harmonize instead of startle. The train ran downward into a beauty that admits romance but is independent of it. Youth demands colour and blue sky, but Martin, turned thirty, longed for Form. Perhaps it is a cold desire, but it can save a man from cynicism; it is a worker's religion, and Italy is one of its shrines. When the glamour of her art and of her nationalism have faded, and the last attempt to exploit her past is over, the Alps will still be on tiptoe for flight, as for Bellini, for Mazzini, the Apennines will still respond across the Lombard Plain.[7] Martin had entered her often before, but never with such sensations; he saw a quality that he would have despised ten years ago. She, like himself, had abandoned sentiment; she existed apart from associations by the virtues of mass and line: her austere beauty was an image of the millennium towards which all good citizens are cooperating.

They passed by hills of dun and lakes of lead. Lady Borlase

was disappointed. Venetia read Jaurès. Presently the young man came, very shy, but determined to pick their brains about Tramonta. Martin looked it up on the map, and advised him to hire a bicycle or a car at Milan.

'And one thing more,' said Lady Borlase: 'you may want a permesso.'

'A permesso is a permission,' explained Venetia.

'None was needed in my day, but owners grow stricter. He lives at Milan – I forget his name: a silk-merchant. You must inquire at your hotel or one of the libraries: they will tell you.'

'Let me get it for you,' said Martin, feeling that he owed the man some civility. 'No trouble. I'm used to permesso-hunting. I'll meet you with it, somewhere tomorrow.'

The other agreed, not very enthusiastically.

'What about the centre of the Galleria – the Arcade? There's no missing that. Meet me there at six p.m. tomorrow.'

Now it was the other's turn. As one who performs a painful duty, he handed Martin his card.

'Thanks very much,' said Martin, and read 'Lieutenant C.P. March' upon it. 'My name's Whitby and our hotel at Milan is the Royal.'

Such was the origin of their friendship.

CHAPTER TWO

Martin Whitby was the son of a Quaker manufacturer. He was attached to his father and all through life they remained friends, but it was his mother who educated him. She sent him to a good day-school, where he gained a scholarship for Cambridge, and before she died saw him established in a character that was both sensitive and strong. He had not grown up in cultivated circles nor had he that aversion to culture that our public schools inspire – a remedy worse than the disease. If, at the age of eighteen, he had no knowledge of literature and art, he had at least no feeling against them. His mind had been prepared for beauty, and as soon as books and pictures and music touched it, it flowered.

After her death he became a sceptic, but without any rendings of heart: indeed the change was more apparent to others than to himself. He gave up Meeting and profitable converse, and went to theatres instead, but it never seemed to him that he had turned away from anything essential, and he gently pardoned his father for gently pardoning him. The chasm between belief and unbelief is not very wide to those who feel religion to be an attitude of mind which may spring from either, and who have not to part with a dogma or wrestle with the sense of sin. Martin crossed more easily than the Anglican or Nonconformist; he lost less (they will say he had nothing to lose), and though he doubted a purpose behind the Universe, he never ceased to act as if there was a purpose. Of course he had his difficulties and temptations; for instance he nearly became a bad citizen. When beauty flowered, the wonder of life so dazzled him that he saw nothing else, and the world appeared as a gymnasium in which fine fellows develop their muscles and swing about from rope to rope. But he had an Englishman's capacity for correcting his faults, and a Quaker's capacity for perceiving them, and he took himself sternly in hand.

This social crisis, which was more acute than the religious, and fixed his character for life, originated in the Miss Borlases. They were the daughters of the Master of the College. Venetia was at Newnham, Dorothea lived at home, and was destined by her parents for a more domestic career. Both were in full revolt against their lot. Their war cry was 'Be tidy'. They wanted to help in tidying up the world. It is time. The age of discovery is over – there will be no new countries. It is time to arrange the old, and all men and women must turn to. Romance, whether in action or thought, is a relic of the age of untidiness; it assumes the unknown, whereas we know, or at all events we know enough. Untidiness. The word caught. It ran like wildfire through Newnham, and drew from Lady Borlase the retort that the lady students were still housemaids at bottom. 'Art and literature are mere untidiness,' cried Venetia. Dorothea corrected her: 'True art and literature will only spring from tidiness.' She had the finer mind, but Martin preferred Venetia. Her crudity inspired him.

Love followed, and it was orderly love. Martin was one of the happy men upon whom Nature plays no tricks. He only loved where he had liked, and if he had not esteemed Venetia he would never have become passionate for her. He never knew what it is to be split in two, for reason to drag one way and passion the other until the victim is red with shame and perhaps black with mud. He regarded such a victim as inexplicably gross, and if, as had once happened, it was one of his own friends, he never felt the same towards the man again. His love for Venetia was not adventurous; it glorified the known; and confirmed philosophy.

Lady Borlase and all sensible people encouraged the match, which took place as soon as he made himself a position. He entered the Civil Service, and a year later his college elected him to a Fellowship. He had not expected the honour, and felt no inclination to give up London and go into residence: Cambridge may be the nursery of winning causes, but it is seldom their home. But he was glad of the status, for no one could object to him marrying the Master's daughter now.

Passion passed in time. For the Whitbys, as for all married people, the sea began to ebb after a few months, and they had to face whatever it uncovered. Now came the critical moment of their career. With what joy did they see the comradeship of the past re-emerging, but softened by a tenderness that had not been in the past. They had produced wedded love. They had solved one modern problem, and if they became a little intolerant to those who had not solved it, if they sometimes forgot that money and outside interests, and a healthy child, had helped them, nevertheless they were receiving the reward of merit; the lustful and the insincere will never be rewarded.

By the time Martin went to Italy, his inner life was complete, and he is submitted as an example of a civilized man. In appearance he was tall and slightly wistful, with a superficial shyness that was deceptive but never treacherous. There he is, standing in the heart of modern Italy, where the two tunnels of the Galleria intersect. His feet are on the central stone. To his right and left are transepts, the nave in front leads out to the blue sky of the square. The caffès round the crossing are deserted: for some high reason it is not their hour. But down the nave a crowd gathers; tourists, merchants, officers, ladies, sip their vermouth or americano, or wait their turn for an empty table. Others lounge at the shops; here are photographs and artistic furniture, and silk pyjamas, and Dante as a paper-weight, and dubious literature and corsets and pianos: here is stuff of the future, still chaotic and unformed, for all its semblance of finish; here, if facts were facts, is the cathedral of Milan. Martin noted the chaos, he noted everything, and was thrilled by nothing.

He was pleased to see the youthful officer of yesterday approaching him. Except when he was on holiday he had no time to spend over ordinary dullish chaps. Then his heart expanded. He liked to be kind to them and to talk their language if he could discover it, and he could do this without feeling superior, for it was his manner not his attitude that altered. But he was to put his foot in it over Mr March.

'That's right,' he said heartily. 'I've found out about your permesso, but I haven't got it yet: I thought we might go together for it now.'

'Oh, you haven't got it.' He seemed disappointed.

'Well, we've been sightseeing, and besides – I have a suggestion to make. That was partly why I put it off. We propose to go to Tramonta as well – and we wondered whether...'

Before he could finish the sentence, the boy had exclaimed 'Oh no' with such vehemence that they both blushed. Then he apologized. He regretted his ungentlemanly speech. It was terrible.

'Yes, yes, of course I understand,' cried Martin, startled and a little mortified. 'Of course. You're travelling alone – I used to. It was only that there would have been a seat in our car if you cared to take it. Please say no more, sir. All we have to do, is to get the permessi made out separately – ours for tomorrow, and yours for when you wish.'

'I can't trouble you now.'

'Oh, come along.' He looked at him. 'Yes, do come along.

We take the Porta Magenta tram, and it'll be done in ten minutes.'

He came, but his own speech had plunged him into bad temper. They passed down the Galleria and in front of the Cathedral.

It was already closed for the night, and, in the brilliant sunshine, had the effect of an eyeless monster, which the good Milanese had decided to preserve. The vast bronze doors, the inscription to Mary in childbirth, the heavy front breaking into sudden fantasy of pinnacles – they belonged to the men who had planned them, not to the men who saw them now. In the piazza, amid cinema-palaces and trams, rose the statue of the Re Galantuomo[8] – the sort of person whom one understands. His horse was shying slightly at the Duomo, his glance was turned to the Galleria that is dedicated to him. 'A Vittorio Emanuele II. I Milanesi.' Like to like.

'And what do you make of the Cathedral?' proceeded Martin. 'It is supposed to be very wonderful. And so it is.' He was thinking of the pedants who have declared it to be not wonderful, but inartistic, finicking, unrestrained – Heaven knows what. The builder who created a mountain system in marble and set the central peak amid highlands of its own – he may have sinned against art, but he has throned the Virgin superhumanly. 'Have you been on the roof? You might see your Tramonta from it – certainly the Alps. – That's our tram –. I went up the first time I came to Italy – nearly ten years ago. Then there was more green, but Lombardy has come on wonderfully. There's a lot of new stuff – factories, workmen's flats, if such things interest you. The plain's speeding up. In another ten years it will be white all over with houses.'

There was no response. Martin regarded him with benevolence, thinking: 'My poor young man, what does it all matter? Do you think we really wanted you to come in our car, or mind you refusing?' They took the tram and descended in a residential quarter of the city, among modern Palazzi. Down a broad street they came to the permesso's abode, and passed through a gateway into a courtyard where oleanders flowered in tubs. It resided on the second floor. Martin rang the bell and a richly furnished flat was opened to their gaze; they saw the Newest Italy – the Italy that is trimming the foothills of the Alps with Byzantine châlets. Everything screamed and shouted and turned into something else; the wallpaper was turkeys and dandelions, the bureau seemed composed of ladies' bodies and its handles of their clothes: two caryatides, supporting nothing, guarded the passage that led from the hall.

The owner of Tramonta was at his caffè, but the servant promised to telephone to him. She added apologetically, 'With permission I close the door.'

'Close it by all means,' said Martin. – 'The flat's an eye-opener, isn't it,' he remarked to his companion, when it was shut in their faces.

'Eye-opener?'

'I meant awful bad taste. Tramonta will be perfect in its way, but the sort of thing its owner really likes is this.'

'I didn't notice anything special.'

Martin looked him full in the face. It was as blank and 'eyeless' as the Duomo. Did he notice or follow anything? Would he look like that if he had to lead his men into action? Then the door was opened again by a girl of fifteen who stared at them impudently.

'Bettin', what are you doing?' cried the servant, who was at the telephone.

'It's so hot – I am letting in the fresh air'; and she vanished between the caryatides.

'What was that?' asked Mr March.

'They were talking Milanese – I think she said it was hot.'

'What's Milanese?'

'The dialect. They always talk it among themselves.'

'Is it hard to follow?'

Here she returned, slapping each of the turkeys on the wallpaper as she came down the passage. 'I hate these birds,' she announced, and flung herself about the hall.

'What is she doing that for?'

'I should say she is showing off, if you ask me.'

'Maria – Marietta – Mariuccia – what do they want, these men?'

'We want to go to Tramonta,' interposed Martin.

'Tramonta?' she screamed, and doubled in two with laughter. 'Tramonta? I hate Tramonta.'

'Bettina, be quiet,' said the servant; 'I cannot hear the papa's voice.'

She was quiet for a moment and then, as if it was her first appearance, addressed the two men. 'Good evening, signorini; Signor Hoeppler is out; will you not come in and wait for him?'

'She's asking us in,' said Martin. 'What's your opinion?'

'I don't mind. Whatever's usual.'

Martin liked accepting invitations, and Bettina and her setting were far from usual. She led the way into a sitting-room, ceaselessly touching her hair. Never for an instant was she quiet, and though she talked to Martin she kept her eyes on his companion.

'Are you foreigners?'

'Yes.'

'English or Americans?'

'English.'

'I hate the English.'

'Why?' inquired Martin. But there was no reason. She was merely spicing the conversation heavily, as indifferent cooks will.

'You talk Italian very – badly, I think,' was her next turn.

'Perhaps, signorina. But with what expression!'

As things were going he thought this a good joke. She heard it without a smile; indeed she never smiled throughout, and beneath the surface gaiety he had the sense of desolation and despair.

'Your friend – cannot he talk Italian too?'

'Not yet.'

'Then he is very stupid.'

'Ah! Is that why you look at him with such sympathy?'

Surely this should have done. But it is not a line in which an ex-Quaker is proficient and Bettina seemed to know this. She pointed to the bookcase, with another screech of Tramonta. It was a brochure this time, issued by an archaeological society. Martin was looking at some reproductions of the frescoes when there was a sound from the front door, and Bettina lifted her hand.

'Dio mio!'[9] she exclaimed. 'We are lost. I hear the papa.'

'Lost, signorina? And why?'

'Stop here,' she whispered. 'You will be safe… he never comes into this room. Do not utter a word. I will go to him and when it is safe I will let you out. Maria… give her a tip…' All her restlessness had vanished. She glided out as softly as a snake.

'I'm not going to stand this,' exclaimed Martin, and promptly followed her. He came across the papa in the hall and stamped upon the ridiculous intrigue before it had begun.

'Do not apologize,' said Signor Hoeppler (enormously fat),

with condescension. 'Many professors of Art go to Tramonta and come for permessi here first. It is necessary.'

'I hate Tramonta,' said Bettina in an exhausted voice.

He waddled into his study. 'Tramonta is one of the glories of Lombardy,' he proceeded. 'Many professors of Art and those who are interested in painting, like yourselves, go there to see the frescoes, many frescoes, and the moat with its drawbridge and the tower – very antique – and the apartments covered with frescoes. But – never without a permesso. That is absolutely necessary. You arrive without a permesso. Our fattore[10] says, "Where is your permesso?" "My permesso? Is one necessary?" "Yes." "Alas, I have no permesso." Then – away!' He stared at them fiercely.

Martin murmured, 'How fortunate we are,' and so on.

'Are we going to get the things?' asked his companion.

'Oh yes, rather.'

'Yes, you are fortunate, for in another week I should have been in the country. My wife and the rest of my family and my servants are there already.'

'Ah, really. They will enjoy the peace of the castle after the noise of the town.'

'The castle?' cried its owner, much offended. 'What castle? My wife at Tramonta? My family spend their August holiday among contadini[11] and mud? What an idea! Old frescoes may interest students, but not for me.'

His opinion on the glory of Lombardy being out at last, he tore some printed forms out of a book, and went to the front door. There Martin drew himself together for the final speech. He repeated his apologies and his gratitude, and his sense of obligation; he thanked Signor Hoeppler in his own name and in his companion's and in his wife's and his mother-in-law's. It was a good speech and he enjoyed making it. Signor Hoeppler too seemed to think him adequate at last, shook him by the hand, and gave the permessi to the servant. Then he retired with his daughter who was still murmuring that she hated something.

'One, two, three, four,' said Maria, counting the tickets. 'Four lire, please. One lira per person.'

'Good Lord!' cried Martin. 'If we haven't got to fork out as well. Yes, it is, it *is* an eye-opener.' He paid what was asked, and the flat and its marvels closed on them forever.

'Not typically Italian,' was his verdict, as they went down the stairs. 'Though whether it mayn't be the Italian of the future –. These Milanese seem to me really peasants gone wrong. Italy has to produce a middle class – every nation that counts has to – and Signor Hoeppler is her first shot at it. She'll do better another time. She's neither poetical nor heroic nor artistic really. She used to be, and still lives on her reputation – hence all this rubbish about frescoes, many frescoes in the antique style. He felt he had to talk like that, though the only things he really cares about are flashy furniture and money. Oh, and that girl! Did you see what she tried to do?'

'No.'

'Made out that we had no business in the flat, though she invited us. When her father came back, she wanted us to hide and then escape by bribing his servant. It's the horror of barbarism with none of its beauty. And yet, all the same, it's the future. I don't believe in people remaining peasants. To stop in the country and look picturesque – it isn't enough.'

It interested him to see the problem so clearly. Italy has produced the worst bourgeoisie in Europe. There is no doubt of it. And yet, from his point of view, it was an advance on anything she had produced before. Theoretical, in spite of his devotion to facts, he worked out her destiny; with her physique and brains she ought to accomplish no end.

He paid little heed to his companion, who had proved altogether too cross and dull. But his exposition of Italy was interrupted by a cold 'excuse me –'. He looked up – they were in the tram – and the blue eyes fixed him severely.

'I must point out,' he said, 'that we have left that girl in the lurch.'

'Bettina? Have we?'

'We have not done as she asked us. We came out of the room when she told us not to, and now her father will be angry.'

'I couldn't do as she told me,' said Martin. 'It was too silly; and I only hope he will be angry with her.'

'Excuse me – we have not behaved like gentlemen.'

Martin was taken aback, but did not retreat. 'I suppose we haven't,' he said. 'For my part I didn't want to.'

'What ever do you mean? I don't understand such a remark.'

'I mean that Bettina was a tawdry silly girl who thought it would be fun to compromise us.'

'What's that to do with us leaving her in the lurch?'

'Everything. I'm not inclined to sacrifice myself for that type.'

'I don't agree.'

Martin determined to read him a lesson. 'So you would have skulked in the sitting-room while she lied to her father, and then bribed his servant to let you out –'

'I don't like any woman to suffer.'

'No more do I. Least of all my wife. It wouldn't have been particularly pleasant for Mrs Whitby if we had behaved as you suggested,' said Martin. 'Gentlemanly behaviour has usually another side to it.'

He cried, 'You twist everything round,' and left the tram, red as fire.

'Unlike me that,' was Martin's reflection, 'I don't generally cross swords, least of all with a boy. But I do hate that pseudo-chivalry so – Venetia does so hate it. It's against all true intercourse with women, and all progress. Why won't Lady Borlase give it up? It must be jumped on, or – Oh, blast! I've forgotten to give him the permesso ticket, and I don't know where his hotel is. Well, he'll call for it when he likes. Young fool.'

CHAPTER THREE

The expedition to Tramonta was the pleasantest they had ever made: all three looked back to it as the crown of their holiday. Everything went right from the first – a perfect car and a perfect chauffeur. By the time they had finished reading their letters from home, they were rushing along a magnificent road, embanked high above the plain, with vines and acacias on either side of them, and the Alps in front.

'– But poor Martin has no letters.'

'Not a letter. Not a figure. Nirvana.'

'The higher mountains will soon be hidden,' said Venetia, who was in great good humour, and unusually civil to natural objects. 'We must look at them all we can.'

'Yes, but if I do, I can't see the people,' said her mother. 'I want to see the people – the unspoilt people working in the fields.'

'I vote we spin this expedition out,' said Martin. He leant forward and said to the chauffeur, 'What is your name?'

'Gemelli, Aristide.'

'Aristide, we want to go slowly.'

'I go at whatever rate you like and in whatever direction, and for any length of time.'

And the car slackened proudly, like a curbed racehorse. For it was one of those days when the Italians have decided to be accommodating. They seem to telegraph the order over the whole peninsula – even to the station-masters – so that the tourist suddenly finds that he has everything he wants and pays for nothing that he does not have. Such days are rarer than they used to be but they still occur, and may persist to the end of time.

'Now the people – Nettie, look at those children. How

beautiful! They seem to be another race,' cried Lady Borlase, struck with the change from the town. Instead of the pasty Milanese workmen, she saw men walking as kings, and treating her like a queen. They were brown and happy and frank; some of them drove their families in carts, on the eastern sides of which green boughs were fixed, for the sun was fierce. But not too fierce: there had been rain in the night, and the watercourses gurgled as in spring.

Martin said: 'I know all about men. I look at mountains.' For Monte Rosa was disappearing behind the foothills; the lower snows had vanished already, and soon there would be no reminder that God can build on so vast a scale. The Alps broke and regrouped as they approached; the sense of a crystalline wall had gone, and they proved to be earth like the plain. But earth most delicately coloured – greys and browns, quiet purples and greens – and the plain with its cabbages of maize and rice-fields and its poplars and plantations of oak, carried on the colouring. Here and there, whatever the crop, rose trellised columns of iron and steel, taller than any tree, and joined at the summits by wires. They were part of the electric light installation system for Milan, and a reminder to Martin, had he needed one, that man will utilize nature in the future as he has in the past. They stretched direct from the mountains to the city.

'How much further is Tramonta?'

'I can't remember,' said Lady Borlase. 'It was in the old time when your father and I went.' She was filled with tender memories of a less eminent and a less tedious Sir Hugh, who had driven with her day after day and had been simple and friendly. Martin reminded her of him – and he had been free from Martin's perverse opinions. 'It was in the old time, before one attempted so much. We just drove about Lombardy, not far from the foot of the hills, and stopped when we wanted to. A very happy unremunerative drive.'

Martin talked to the chauffeur.

'Don't distract him,' advised Venetia. 'There are so many ditches. Oh, what a pleasant day! What a very enjoyable drive.'

They had entered into a by-road, sunk deep in the country's bosom. The mountains had disappeared behind trees and crops of maize, and the sense of direction went with them. 'We are really lost at last,' said Lady Borlase. 'Nettie, what steps do you propose to take? Fie! It is no moment to enjoy when all around is so untidy. Tidy it up, Nettie! To your life's work. Have you forgotten all you learned at Newnham?'

Uncertain whether to say 'Yes, I have' or 'No, I haven't', Venetia said nothing, but she smiled, and her mother smiled back at her. The car now splashed through mud, and its educated occupants bounced up and down on the cushions with humorous cries of pain. 'One suffers, eh?' cried Aristide. 'But we have arrived.' And he drew up in a broad clearing, half piazza and half farmyard.

'No, we've not,' said Martin. 'Where's my medieval castle, very antique, with a tower?'

'Yes, we have,' said his mother-in-law. 'This is Tramonta. I remember it. – It's in there.'

She pointed to a wall of cottages. There was a door in the middle of it at which the chauffeur knocked. No one opened it, but information gradually accumulated. The fattore was away – he alone had the key – he was at the other end of the estate trying to mend a bridge. It was a curious scene, for the cottages seemed equally unable to get out or to let anyone in: they screamed through barred windows, while their babes waved pods of Indian corn. Other labourers gathered round the car, and Aristide selected the cleanest of these for a guide.

Bearing a pitchfork, the delighted man mounted on the front seat, and on they went, and returned with the fattore on their knee. In what other country could three gentlefolk, a bailiff, a farm-labourer, and a smartish chauffeur, eat the bread of angels together? Will not Italy solve every problem if she has solved this?

And now the door was unlocked, and the jollity of the day was, for Martin, tinged with Romance. He moved into a half-forgotten world. He saw a castle, beautiful indeed in form and substance, but recalling some higher beauty. Where had he dreamt of such a place? Vague memories of Monsalvat or Asgard[12] – and he who despised such allusions! – vague memories of all the strongholds that have been manned by Virtue, came to him as he crossed a bridge and entered the dark red doorway. Italian in detail, Tramonta had drawn its conception from the feudal north, and its bricks sang of chivalry and the crusades. In its courtyard were faded frescoes of the sixteenth century, but by a happy chance they represented the war between Christendom and the Turks, and the victory of the former at Lepanto[13]. The final gleam! Cardinals blessing, galleys charging, infidels falling by thousands into the scarlet sea. With what enthusiasm had they been painted, and now only the birds saw them.

'I will show you everything,' said the fattore. 'I will open every window and let in the sun. Then you shall climb the tower and then you shall go out by the drawbridge.'

'Do so. Here are the permessi.'

He waved his hand. 'I am master here. You need no permessi, for I take you. And now let us begin.'

Tramonta was a fortress inside a fortress of cottages: they had been built on some outer line of defence; and by a complicated system of doors and barriers each had its own connections with the world. The arrangement was rational enough – Signor Hoeppler did not want the farm children to go playing among his cocoons – and yet it produced enchantment. The fattore, justly proud, explained it to his visitors – how the men they saw out of the windows were really very far away, very; how no one could enter the castle except with this one key, how thousands of lire – though they might not think it – were represented in its deserted rooms. He showed them silk in every stage, and dried vegetables and piles of seed corn, and always, as he had promised, he opened the windows. Horsemen and pages and ladies, and here a walled city, wonderfully distinct, and there Tramonta itself, as it looked in the days of its glory, and Nymphs to signify fields, and Tritons to signify the sea, and ceilings of pure decoration – the light fell upon all from squares of blue. Dust arose as they tramped, till the wealth of the place seemed fabulous. They were shown and remembered Tramonta not as an antique, but as a treasure-house where half the wealth of Lombardy lay stored. Could we but capture it and use the wealth rightly! Could we but nourish not Bettina and her father but the starving armies of the Lord.

The frescoes were of little note artistically and the names of the painters – Pietro Modenese, Ignazio Malpaga and the rest – had only been unearthed by recent research. In Lady Borlase's time they had been by no one – a preferable arrangement; they had sprouted like lichen from the walls. Now an earnest tourist could have been tiresome, for it was possible to distinguish between one painter and another from internal evidence. But Venetia was not in the mood, and wandered like her companions through a haze of beauty, seeing what she was, and not craning her neck for what was painted in dark passages. The best were in a room on the first floor; they came to them towards the end of their visit, as they descended from the tower. The view from it had appealed to Martin's earlier sense of beauty as well as to his later. Form had wedded colour and behind their union stood Romance, blessing it; that is where Romance should stand – not in the foreground whither incompetent boys would lug her. He felt so happy as he came down the stairs and so efficient. He knew himself to be clever and kind and moral and energetic, and to be surrounded by friends who were like him. He knew this – without self-consciousness and without conceit: the truth – for it was one – lay in his soul like a star.

'And now,' the fattore was saying, 'I will open these windows also.' Martin followed him into the room, and the light fell upon a fresco of the usual type. Soldiers were going out to battle, or perhaps down to the sea to embark on the red-oared ships. They marched in loose order with their faces turned towards the spectator; some of them were portraits, others idle reminiscences of Raphael; all were instinct with the swagger of their century. They marched against a background of grey-brown hills over which were scattered villagers firing cannon. A victory flew above them, and a Roman helmet, for which they had no use, lay negligently upon a grassy knoll. Martin at the first glance cried out excitedly.

'What's wrong?' asked his wife.

'It's extraordinary – it's that man – he; that man in the train who wouldn't come with us.'

Lady Borlase said: 'Which of them? How amusing.'

'Which? Why, the young one of course with the baton.'

'Do you see any likeness, Nettie?'

'They both have fair hair, but I should have said that's all.'

'No, no, the spirit, the expression...'

'The expression is quite different, my dear Martin. Master

Lieutenant March who didn't think our company good enough – Master March was reserved, one might even say Superior. But this man is fiery, or as fiery as the painter can make him.'

'No, you're wrong. It's only an accident that fire – it's what he can look like when –' He stopped himself. 'It's he. That's why he came to Milan. Between him and this picture there's some link. – Venetia, do look.'

'Perhaps an ancestor,' said Venetia, following her mother.

'Oh, wait a bit – if he is, it's three hundred years at least.'

Venetia alluded to Mendelism[14], her mother said with a touch of pride, 'Sir Hugh's family goes back further than that; he has a tree that he delights to show, but I thought you all despised such vanities.' They both passed out of the room, having enjoyed the general effect, and the fattore prepared to close the shutters.

'One moment, please,' said Martin, and wrote a few notes in his guidebook to impress the picture on his memory. It touched him strangely. It was not the work of a good artist, no nor of a sincere one, but the wall on which it was painted – that was sincere and shone through it. He wrote, 'very moving: warriors about to fight for their country and faith', and was amazed at what he had written, so little resemblance did it bear to his usual art criticisms. Another hand might have guided his pencil. Having sketched the coat of arms that hung on a tree, he gave the signal, and the shutters were closed. The warriors and their leader receded into darkness until Signor Hoeppler should allow them to be shown again.

'Dark, dark as death,' said the fattore gaily. 'When there is light – one sees; when there is none –' he clicked his fingers.

'Exactly,' answered Martin.

For that was the wonder of the picture – that he was here to see it. He might have been at the Basle hospital – or nowhere; he might have been clicked out of life. But he was here: a fellow creature had saved him.

In vain he struggled with his emotion, knowing it to be weakening; no true vision has ever come through the might-have-been. As long as he stayed in Tramonta the vision persisted. He saw neither the man nor the picture but a power behind both, to which he could give no name. That power had saved his life. It was about to mangle Turks by the thousand and throw them into the sea. Nothing that he had experienced described it, and when the emotion passed it left him with feelings of ignorance and shame.

'I left March's permesso with our Hall Porter, with a note,' he remarked. 'I do hope he will call for it: it was the best I could do.'

'If it's an ancestor, he will,' said Venetia. 'He's the type who cares about Family, and prefers a bad portrait of an ancestor to a good portrait of someone else. I'm glad he didn't come with us and spoil our day.'

'Or we his perhaps.'

He was anxious to talk about the man. He held no brief, and was willing to hear him blamed, but he wanted him discussed, for the castle belonged to him and needed his interpretation. He liked it rather less than he had. There was a touch of snobbery about it. Its heroes were all gentlemen, fighting for upper-class homes, and it ignored the sweaty galley-slaves who really won Lepanto. 'I am in a place,' he said, 'of which my little mind does not wholly approve.' Venetia agreed, but it is impossible to communicate emotion: the soul is obliged to keep her secrets whether she wishes to or not.

The fattore let them out by the drawbridge, as he had promised. A great slab of wall fell outwards at his touch, and bridged a moat. They saw across the outer yard, through an arch in the barrier of cottages, and then straight into the country, down a track that had once been a princely approach. It was a worthy exit. They passed out into the common world. The others began to talk about the farm-babies, but Martin looked back. This was the main entrance, severe and heroic, guarding a well of gold. He imagined himself arriving three centuries earlier, probably as a monk of sorts, and demanding hospitality. He would be well treated, so long as he knew his place. But if he was impertinent or heretical, woe betide him. As he imagined, the fattore set his simple machinery in motion. The drawbridge rose up, and Tramonta shut.

CHAPTER FOUR

The excursion ended as pleasantly as it had begun. They drove forward to the hills and lunched on rising ground among chestnuts. Then they made straight for Milan, while the giants rose up behind them in afternoon formation: the westerly spurs were coated with bloom, but in the east new delicacies had arisen. They merged again into a crystalline wall: then the wall became a girdle, too precious to rest on the earth, with blue sky above it and blue haze below. Milan thickened: square white houses dashed by the car, as if an ocean was nearing; then formed into ignoble froth. But as long as the vista was clear, the Alps rose at the end of it, and when they were hidden from men the Madonna on the Cathedral spire still saw them.

Mr March had not fetched his note, but, by bad luck, he arrived just after they did. Venetia saw him in the hall and they had an unfortunate little conversation together.

'Oh, here you are!' she cried in her tactless way. 'I know what you've come for. I'll get it you. Here it is. And do tell me: is it your portrait there or not?'

'My portrait?' he cried, looking as if he'd seen a ghost.

'My husband swears it is: don't you, Martin? You say it must be some ancestor of Mr March's.'

'Oh, I don't know,' murmured Martin, feeling that some new sense had descended upon him that afternoon. Venetia ought never to have mentioned his theory, never.

'Why, you were so keen upon it. You said he had come specially to see it. Mr March, is it so?'

Looking her straight in the face the boy said, 'I'm told so.'

'One for you, Martin.'

Martin was watching her victim; in fact he felt a victim

himself. He was rather nervous, for March had a queer temper. He saw him flush and look disgusted. 'They are making a genealogical tree of our family and wanted me to go and Kodak that picture,' he said.

'A genealogical tree that *is* genealogical would be valuable,' said Venetia severely. 'But people are so apt to make a fuss about their eminent ancestors, if they have any, and to hush up those who aren't. I know by my father. When he talks of "family" he means only his grandmother's family. On the other sides he was nothing, and this gives a false view. Martin – you were saying that there's no such thing as "family" in England. The population has intermarried too much. Let me see: if you go back to the tenth generation hasn't each of us over a thousand ancestors, and it isn't likely all of them were Dukes.'

'Those ancestors themselves may have intermarried,' said Martin. 'A thousand is too large an estimate.'

'Still you agree in essentials.' Having delivered herself of the faith that was in her, she sat down. Mr March had gone.

'It's a tactless little wifey,' said Martin, perching on the edge of her chair.

'I wasn't tactless. I knew it would annoy him all the time. It is a great great pity when boys think about family, and I was glad to have the opportunity of taking it out of him.'

'I'm half inclined to respect everybody's thoughts.'

'That's floppy, Martin. Some thoughts are harmful to the community. If he misreads the past, how can he read the present? Let him keep to his soldiering and mountaineering.'

'He is keeping to them. That's what we resent. I say again: it's an atmosphere of which my little mind does not approve. It's the Tramonta theory.'

'Anyhow it's a wrong one.'

'But held how passionately, age after age.'

'Oh, if you go in for passion! If the strength of a feeling is to be the test of its goodness, all murderers go top at once.'

'Granted. That's why I don't go in for it.'

'I'm not so conceited as to suppose I should do him any direct good. But I may have given him something to think about, and next time he comes across our type, they may influence him. Most work is done indirectly. Educationalists like Dorothy[15] admit as much. They try to drop knowledge into the subconscious stratum of the child's mind.'

Martin blew out his cheeks. 'Here we come up against my great argument with Dorothy. I maintain that such knowledge must itself be dropped subconsciously. A child, even a young lieutenant, is a sharper subject than you school ma'ams suppose. He sees through you. You try to touch his depths without using *your* depths, and it can't be done. One subconsciousness must call to another. Which is a clumsy way of saying that there must be affection.'

'Affection subconscious?'

'Oh God. I don't know. We've got such a cold grey language. We ought to be talking poetry, not psychology. I give it all up.'

Venetia loved to have something to bite on. This intellectual bout with her husband made a climax to a very pleasant day. She leant back in her cane chair, and wondered which of them was right. If she could decide, it would really help her to help people. A little drowsy with motoring, she tried to estimate the force of family pride, to classify the emotion ethically, and to locate the stratum that produces affection. She nodded. She woke up to hear Martin saying quite crossly, 'Venetia! Oh damnation.'

He held in his hand the permesso, torn in two. He had picked it up in the porch of the hotel, where March had thrown it. 'He's not going at all!' he cried. 'We've put him off.'

'I'm very sorry indeed,' she exclaimed. 'It's no fault of ours, but I am very very sorry.'

'Don't be sorry,' said her mother, whom they had supposed to be absorbed in the paper. 'You have clearly influenced him for good, and he is repentant.'

'But Martin, what has happened?'

'We've spoilt Tramonta for him. He can't stand us. He'll never go there now, although it belongs to him.'

'Not stand us?'

'He ought to be able to stand us but he can't.'

CHAPTER FIVE

Lady Borlase never planned her holidays. She took plenty of money to a likely place, and then saw what happened. This time it ended in a motor tour. The summer was cool, and free from dust, and they were able to hire the Tramonta car and its chauffeur for a fortnight. They went along the Emilian Way to Modena, stopping at towns they had been too idle to visit from the train, and then they careered for a time among the Apennines.

It was a pleasant holiday, but did not come up to their expectations. Rain fell. Flaws developed both in the chauffeur and the car. Aristide proved far from perfect. He overslept, was unpunctual, and – though this was not his fault – he suffered from lameness. The garage had not told them this, and they had not found it out as long as he sat majestically enthroned. But as soon as he descended, life became painful for him and slow for them. They were obliged to save him in every possible way, and he was willing that they should do so. Martin fetched and carried. Venetia went into wineshops. As for the car, it was a bad hill-climber.

Martin would not have minded these trifles if he had been happy in himself. But there had been some tiny jar among his nerves, and he felt insipid. The cathedrals and bastioned cities of the Emilia seemed built not only by other hands but for other eyes to look at. Romance blessed them no longer, and though he reminded himself that it is better thus – else would beauty sink into the picturesque – he longed for that moment at Tramonta, where he had gathered up all the threads of joy. Beauty may sink into the decorative too – she moves between two abysses – and this Italian tour gave him the sense of stage scenery which borrows all its value from the events that take place in front of it. No events did take place – here was the defect. The jar inside him was spiritual as well as aesthetic: he was rushing day after day through a world that did not belong to him.

Until the crisis came – and there was to be one – he scarcely realized that anything was amiss, and Lady Borlase found him merely a little quieter than usual. Venetia noticed no change – she had not a noticing disposition – and she was surprised when her mother spoke. It was at Modena. Tippy as ever, Martin had avoided the tourist hotel and taken them to one that was patronized by the University, stately and clean, and Lady Borlase overflowed with gratitude, and remarked, 'Nettie, you and I are a very lucky pair of petticoats.'

Venetia deprecated this vein in her mother, and tried to change the subject.

'Whether Martin is equally lucky, I doubt,' she continued. 'I wish he had a man to go about with.'

'What could a man do that we don't do?'

'He could be a man, my dear.'

'Well, as you know, I don't agree at all, and no more does Martin. He hates what we call "smoking-room civilization". He's as anxious as I am that Hugo shouldn't be taught all the rubbish about "little girls do this" and "little boys do that". If he likes people – that's all he cares about.'

'No doubt that's the correct attitude, but I has my feelings. He'd be happier if there was another man.'

'Well, there's the chauffeur. Or did you mean a gentleman?' she added with a touch of scorn.

'Heaven help me, but I did mean a gentleman.'

'Oh.'

'Be it how it may, I'm afraid he's not enjoying motoring as much as we are. Don't you think he isn't as merry as usual.'

'Everyone has their ups and downs,' said Venetia. 'Sometimes I'm not merry.'

Lady Borlase gave a clap of laughter.

'What is it, mother?'

'Dearest Nettie, nothing.'

'I believe you're laughing at me. Did I say anything odd?'

It was at moments like these that Lady Borlase saw the unalterable candour of her soul. 'Anyhow I'm merry,' she said. 'I'm a vulgar old trot, and I want Martin to be the same.'

'I expect he's thinking of his work. I'll ask him.'

When asked, Martin admitted that he was. He had linked himself again to the files in Whitehall, and had been writing a telling letter in his mind while his eyes had rested on the incomparable menagerie of stone lions that crouch round the portals of Modena Cathedral. That was it. He *had* been thinking of his work. His spirits rose at the discovery, and when Venetia remarked that he ought to make this a real holiday, he agreed. She did not dwell on the subject, for it seemed of slight importance to her, and she only spoke to please her mother. But the dinner was particularly pleasant, as though the jarring nerves had been composed at last. When it was over he announced that he should take Aristide to a cinematograph entertainment.

He found the chauffeur in a gloomy underworld of menials, tired with cleaning the car, but too polite to refuse the invitation. They left the hotel in pouring rain. It was before the days of special cinema-palaces – those apparitions of cream and electric light that have arisen in Modena and all the world – and the performance took place in a disused shop. The gloomy hum burrowed into Martin's brain like an insect. The art of the future! He did not honestly love it. Fearful of being superior, he laughed and chatted and was rewarded by something sufficiently comic. A kitchen chimney smoked, and a man came to stick it together with glue. Various people came to see him stick it, and the glue-pot upset and stuck the people together instead. They fell over the edge of the roof like a string of caterpillars. Then the fire-escape [*sic*] played on them and they unstuck. It was a far cry from this to Dorothea Borlase and her Morris Dances. It was a far cry either to art or nature. Still it made one laugh, and Aristide thumped his employer on the knee. Then followed a sentimental piece – a child, of American extraction, said his prayers, and afterwards rescued his father and mother from a gang of desperadoes. The atmosphere here was Protestant, but it passed. Then 'The Gaities of Divorce' – a poor set of films, full of bubbles and streaks of lightening [*sic*], representing the same set of models who had been stuck together by the glue. Insidious distortion of life, unfused by the imagination! It seemed to Martin that it must do infinite harm, and that the dreams of the moralist and the poet were guttering down together into a blur.

Then the crisis came.

The film now was a 'Fantasia'. A little boy had fallen asleep to dream of ghosts. Chairs and curtains came alive, and though the horror was mechanical it seemed the more horrible to Martin for that. Profoundly depressed, he watched the cinematograph's version of the spirit world. There was no beauty in it, no mystery. First the washstand rolled its eyes and then the wardrobe, and then the coal-scuttle. The little boy, duly alarmed, stood up. As he did so, there was an explosion. He and his ghosts disappeared, and the room, Martin's room, was filled with smoke: the film had caught on fire.

He found himself outside in the street.

How he had got there, he did not know; he tried

immediately to re-enter. But the crowd surged out after him, the matchboard of the passage broke, those who were waiting in the vestibule fled before him. He was carried out across the arcade into the rain. They were shovelled into the quiet street as from a pit in Hell, and through the arch he could see smoke and flame, and faces swirling out. He tried to beat up against them. Impossible. He had missed the tide.

He shouted in English, 'Take care – he's lame – I've left a lame man in there.' He fought and raged, he had courage to perform wonders, but the particular moment for them had gone by, no one wanted him now. The fire-engine streamed water into the scarlet maw. No one was hurt, except by panic, and at last among the outcoming faces he saw the chauffeur's, not hurt at all.

But it was too late for Martin. The primitive man in him had been roused, and he could not still it. He broke loose and ran like a criminal, shaken by tearless sobs. 'Oh my God, I've been a coward,' he repeated. 'Oh my God you can't forgive that – you never did – you never will.' He would stop suddenly, in the midst of a dark and silent street, and recast. He had left his guest, his social inferior who trusted him; he had left the weak to be trampled under, because he was afraid. He, who believed he had solved life's grosser problems, who had steered so cleverly through religion and work and love, had been toppled base upward in a moment, and could never trust himself again. Here was the Cathedral, magnificent, silent, with lions at its portals. Not for him! He had always assumed he was brave – Englishmen do – had never trained or tested himself, had led a life where bravery is not wanted. In the Army or at sea he would have been unmasked long ago, but he had slipped from one shelter to another, from home to Cambridge, from Cambridge to a Government Office. He had never felt the rough winds that still blow about the world. He imagined them abolished – as by some international agreement! Well, the least breath from them, the merest puff, had touched him this evening, and he had run away.

Half an hour later he went back to the hotel. He was still the same person, and what was sound in him must set to work and fill up this flaw.

They had gone to bed, and Venetia was asleep when he reached her room. He began to undress, looking at himself gravely in the glass. Presently he called her by name.

'Hullo!' she said drowsily. 'You back?'

'Have you heard what happened?'

'Oh yes – film caught fire. Aristide said he saw you, so I didn't sit up.'

'Have you realized what I did?'

She yawned. He sat down on the bed beside her. 'I've been a coward. When the explosion came I thought only of myself. I left him to be killed.'

'But he wasn't killed,' said Venetia, collecting herself. 'He's gone to bed.'

'He might have been.'

'Oh, might –!'

'It's a serious thing I'm telling you. I've been a coward, a coward –'

Venetia woke up, quite. 'Oh, don't begin that! What have you done?' she said sharply.

'When it exploded, I jumped over the people and got out.'

'Oh, lost your head, you mean.'

'Yes.'

'You're no good at an emergency, Martin. You never were. I don't see the use of worrying.'

'Never was? Do you mean you knew?'

'Oh yes. Dorothy pointed it out to me years ago. When a thing comes suddenly you start back. You can't help it. It's ridiculous to call it cowardice. It's merely something physical. It's merely your reflex action, working slower than most people's. People can snatch things out of your hand before you can summon your will to close it up, and that's what happened this evening. The half-penny press may call it cowardice, but we don't.'

'I've got a will, then.'

'Of course.'

'But it always arrives ten seconds too late.'

'Yes, but in ninety-nine cases out of a hundred, ten seconds is *not* too late. In all the important affairs of life there is this ten seconds' interval for deciding.'

Martin was impressed, but not comforted. 'There wasn't this evening,' he remarked.

'There was nothing to decide. Aristide got out as safely without you as he would have with you.'

Martin could not help laughing. 'Venetia, you're a female really, though you mayn't sound like one. My dear, you're all over the place, and all you care about is to comfort your husband who's a coward.'

Venetia cried indignantly: 'Don't talk rubbish. I shouldn't spare you if you deserved it, but I don't consider you deserve it, and nothing will persuade me. No doubt they'd call you a coward in story-books, and mothers' meetings, where there's conventional psychology; but were you a coward that two years' quarrel with my father? That's what I count. Have you ever done what you think wrong in the office?'

'Never. In an office I'm admirable.'

'Don't mention this to mother.'

'Exactly. Exactly.'

'Oh, idiot!' cried his lady, striking him. 'I mean because an accident or the possibility of one make [*sic*] her nervous.'

Martin looked down at her, and the bitterness died out of his smile. He was filled with thankfulness because he had not married what is known as a womanly woman. Had she been of Lady Borlase's type, she would never have forgotten this evening, however much she might have pitied and made allowances for him. But Venetia would forget it – there was not the slightest doubt. It would go clean out of her mind, and perhaps he might forget it too.

At last he said: 'I agree. It was not cowardice.'

Yet he could not forget altogether. Though not cowardice, it was a deplorable flaw, and Venetia had not explained it away. There was – to use her words – this unexpected slowness of the will. How to quicken it up? He had no idea, nor could she help him. In the midst of his gratitude he was conscious of her limitations. There were tangles in life unguessed by her tidy mind. There was – how should one express it? – Tramonta.[16]

CHAPTER SIX

When Clesant left Milan, he went for a few days to some friends in Switzerland, and then travelled direct to the north of England, walking over the moors in the early morning, and reaching his home in time for prayers. He saluted the women of his household – his mother first: she was like him to look at, fair and severe. She was very thin, held herself erect, and was dressed in black, but fashionably: there was something of the Abbess about her, and something of the grande dame. She kissed him without emotion and told him that his Uncle Arthur was there. He replied, 'Oh good,' and turned to his sisters, Olive and Joan.

'We thought you were never coming,' said the former. 'Uncle Arthur's here. He stopped a day longer to see you.'

'Why didn't you come last night?' asked Joan.

'I missed the connection.'

'Why, we expected you last night. Lance drove to meet you in the dogcart. He got back very late, and he's still in bed.'

'He's tired poor Diamond too,' said Olive, who was eighteen but spoke with a baby voice, 'so that Diamond can't take me and Joan to tennis at the Robins'.'

'I don't mind much,' said Joan. 'One meets a bad style there.'

'If Lance can arrange it, you might have the pair,' said Mrs March.

'Oh mother – the pair! How delightful!'

'Though I cannot see the advantage of driving so far to meet people of whose style you disapprove. It is childish. Let us go in to prayers. – Did you enjoy your holiday, Clesant?'

'Yes, thanks. Are you quite fit, mother?'

'Yes, thanks.'

'And everything all right?'

'As far as I know. Ring for the servants, Olive.'

Olive rang, and then a great bell was heard above them, to give notice to anyone in the garden. It filled the narrow chasm in which the house was built, and silenced the noise of the river. 'Oh, I must have a wash,' said Clesant, retreating.

'I would have waited, had you told me. Now Olive has rung the bell.'

A man with a lean keen face joined them. 'Hullo, back?' he remarked, shaking hands as he went to the table. He did not convey the impression of having stopped on to see his nephew.

'Uncle Arthur, neither of the naughty boys will be at prayers.'

'Olive, don't – Uncle Arthur's reading his letters. Clesant, do you want to take yours and Lance's up?'

'Not Lance's,' said her mother. 'If Lance cannot be punctual he can wait. My spectacles. Tell him to make some provision for fetching your luggage from the station. He manages the stables now.'

'And manages them well,' said Mr Vullamy, who heard everything, and modified the tone of the conversation when it was faulty. 'Lance has a light hand for beast and man, but when he comes down, he comes down.'

'Yes, Armstrong's been sacked,' said Joan in an awed voice.

'Old Armstrong?' cried her brother. 'Well, that must have been a tough job. Whatever for?'

His mother remarked that if he was going he had better go. Taking his letters he left the room as the servants entered it. He felt quite happy. A warmer greeting would have disturbed him, for he disliked anything unusual. Distinctly conservative, and too young to have perceived growth or decay, he liked people to be always the same and to do the same things: it was his test of merit. Olive had always looked coyly over her shoulder from babyhood: his mother had always read prayers without emotion, and he could hear her now through the door. She was expounding the unseen. The girls said 'Amen' musically, the servants respectfully; his uncle did not pronounce the syllables, but gave the gruff 'Ain' that comes best from a man, and that Clesant himself would have given. He liked home the better for his absence. Enemies he had always known the world contained, but the last few months had revealed a more puzzling class – people who, without being hostile, did not agree with him. He had met them in large quantities abroad and even at Aldershot, and he did not know how to class them. No doubt he would class them soon, but it was sweet to be in a place where they did not come, sweet to hear falling water and see rocks and trees in their old position, and tread on skins of his father's shooting.

At the top of the stairs he met with a contrast. His mother and her atmosphere were only part of his life, and the other part burst on him in typical fashion. The bathroom door opened, and his elder brother sprang into the passage without a stitch of clothing on him. 'Cles!'

'Dying Gladiator!, that's how it is,' replied [*sic*] Lance, who was reading for the Classical Tripos. Then he imitated other antiques – he was Laocoon with a towel for snakes,[17] or the Apollo Belvedere, or a 'Roman matron of the period of Titus', with a sponge on his head. Clesant, unequal to the situation and to most of the allusions, could only repeat that here was madness and that the servants would be up from prayers in a moment. But he was laughing too much to have any effect; and he knew that his brother really behaved thus because he was glad to see him again; they were devoted to each other.

'My bath's all ready – you can have it. Go on in – you're shocking dirty. I'll get your clean togs from your room. I was going for my own as I heard mother through the floor.'

'All right.' But when he reached the bath, he recoiled in horror, for steam rose out of it. 'You've never given up the cold tub?' he exclaimed.

'Yes, I have,' Lance retorted. 'Only kids take cold tubs now. Of course you wouldn't have heard.'

'A hot bath in summer...' The new idea burst on him with painful suddenness: he was shocked.

'It isn't enervating, 'pon my word, and I like it.'

'Well, get into the beastly thing; I won't.'

'I say, Cles,' he remarked, as he sponged himself, 'don't do this again, I mean don't go again next vac. For instance I didn't know whether to cut down the ash trees in the drive.'

'What did mother want?'

'That's it; she asked me to decide, and I cut them and I think she's disappointed.'

'I wish she had said which she wanted.'

'So do I,' replied Lance, smiling frankly, 'but she wants me to decide, seeing as I'm full-grown and Uncle Arthur's going to make an eldest son of me.'

'Make an eldest son.'

'Ass! It's a phrase. Instead of leaving part of his oof to me and part to you, he's going to leave it all to me, in hopes I ripen into a landed gentry. This is English, quite English, you know. Primogeniture. Large estates. The younger son comes down to the old home now and then for a weekend, but that's sufficient.'

'I hear you've sacked Armstrong. Did you do that off your own bat too?'

'Yes, I did – don't talk about that now. Then Uncle Arthur's settled my profession too. I'm to be a publisher and diddle authors. That will entail – will ultimately entail a house in town, and I shall ask you to my rottener dinner parties.'

'Buck up out and pull the plug.'

'Haw! I never do buck up in these days. I lie in the hot water and get late for prayers.'

'Well, you won't now I'm back.' Seizing the chain he pulled, and though Lance avenged himself by squeezing water into the bowl of his pipe, he won a victory. When the pernicious liquid had run away, he let in the cold, and washed off the stains of travel. It was delicious: none of the baths he had commanded in foreign hotels could touch it, for the supply here came from their own river.

'So I'm fixed up,' continued the other, as he shaved himself: the bathroom was dedicated to the boys by their mother's decree, and they met in it almost daily when they were at home. Olive and Joan had to be content with cans. 'I take my degree next June, and then –' He slashed with his razor at the invisible world.

'I'm fixed up too, if it comes to that.'

'No, you're not. You're half asleep. Some day you'll wake and –' He slashed again. It occurred to neither brother to ask what he was slashing at. They had been trained to believe in some viewless enemy, who would manifest himself in due season.

'I know there's a frightful lot to be done,' said Clesant, feeling immature and stupid.

'Quite so – beginning with breakfast. But keep quiet half a minute, will you.' And without further preface, he knelt down by the side of his bath and said his prayers. He prayed open-eyed, and with the same simplicity that had sent him across the passage without his clothes on, reciting the Lord's Prayer, the Creed, and a private prayer of his own, which rather troubled him, for he wanted little that he had not got, and sometimes could think of nothing to say. His brother, after a moment's hesitation, knelt down too. When Lance was with him, he lost self-consciousness, and those who are inclined to criticize the quality of Lance's orison, may reflect on this. He rose full of thankfulness and gratitude, and better able to play his part in the world.

They were late for breakfast. Their mother said nothing, but Clesant, who could not help his unpunctuality, had a little pot of fresh tea served to him, while Lance was given stewy: he might command the stables, but she remained mistress in her own house. Joan, who had a strong sense of justice, also tried to snub him, and to drag Clesant forward: it was clearly Clesant's turn.

'It was dear of him to go to see Sir Adam's picture, Olive, wasn't it?' she remarked.

'It's not a picture but a fresco,' said Clesant, rather shortly. 'I have brought you a photograph of it, but I have not seen it. I decided not to.'

'Oh, but you went specially to Milan.'

'It is a long way out of Milan. There's a pamphlet about the place that will tell you more than I can.'

'How funny men are! They have no curiosity,' was Olive's contribution.

'But why didn't you go? You're as idle as Lance.'

'I decided.'

'Joan!' said her uncle.

She looked up, pleased and a little startled. It was not often that Mr Vullamy addressed her: he was a man of few words where women were concerned, though the words were always kind.

'This omelette aux champignons – good: it's a good omelette. Can I have the recipe, or is it a state secret?'

'Oh, Uncle Arthur, of course! I'll write it out for you, I shall get it so much clearer. You take the eggs –' Then Olive joined in, and both became agitated: the girls of the family were in every respect inferior to the men. Lance also interfered, describing how he cooked omelettes at Cambridge, and in half a dozen sentences had captured the conversation. He had so many assets. He was large handsome strong, clean of body, kind of heart, with a good brain and a powerful will, both of which he kept in the background. Who wants more? Have we not here the perfect public-school man? Perhaps, but to those who do want more, Lance presented an undignified and charming smile which came from the depths of his being. The whole man danced out through teeth and eyes and wrinkles at the least provocation. He laughed at his own jokes and other people's and at any rot that came along. It wasn't a keen sense of humour – none of the Marches had that: it was something more profound, akin to passion. Mr Vullamy's laugh, though genial enough when he had decided on it, was never prodigal. Clesant laughed seldom, his mother never, the girls only when they were laughed at. Lance alone had the key to men's hearts. He only had to say, 'I say, is there room?' at the door of a railway carriage to make everyone welcome him. Ordinary people liked him because he was what a young gentleman ought to be, and superior people, who complained that there was nothing against him and therefore nothing in him, thawed to his smile. A fire, not sinister, filled him, and even his mother found herself wishing that she had let him have fresh tea. But she checked the wish: she must not spoil her son or allow him to be victorious at Monkswear.

After breakfast, Mr Vullamy took his nephews into the

garden, and made Clesant talk about Switzerland. It was a dull account, but he had an instinctive sympathy with dullness: as far as he could judge, the boy was shaping properly, had been up that chimney and this arête, had enjoyed it in spite of the rain, was modest and hardy. Lighting his pipe he said: 'Climbing is a fine training for the muscles and the eye. And it's a discipline. I'm glad you like it. The best officer, the best leader in any line, will have something of the climber about him, I mean the mountain-climber. It's a discipline for those who are obliged to command. It'll be a bad day for England when men of your age give up the mountains, and take to vagabondage, walking tours, that rot. It disintegrates, disintegrates. A walking tour is merely for a weekend. Charles Kingsley was against them, and there is no doubt that – though he was unfitted for an intellectual duel with Newman – Kingsley's opinions are always sound at the core.[18]

'Why did he not approve of walking tours, Uncle Arthur?'

'His opinion was that they encouraged introspection.'

'Damned true that!' exclaimed Lance. 'I mean as far as my experience goes which of course is limited. A socialist stumped over our country last month, with pamphlets to prove that there is no God.'

'Exactly.'

'If a man is so unfortunate as to be an unbeliever, he might at least keep it to himself.'

'Yes indeed,' said Clesant, from the uncle's other side.

'Fortunately mother did not hear of it – he left pamphlets all over the village – sickening.'

Mrs March had heard of it and had told her brother. But it was part of their plan that Lance should protect her, and they had left him to fight the pamphlets single-handed.

'I tracked the man – sort of paper-chase – and earthed

him up on Bramley Down. "Look at you messing up the jolly country," I told him, and showed a great handful – I'd taken them from under the door-knockers. Yet he seemed a decent sort of man. "Class jealousy –" I told him it was. Of course they can argue.'

'What did he say?' asked his brother.

'His line was that I was really more of an atheist than he was.'

Mr Vallamy murmured, 'How well one knows that line.' Then turning to Clesant, who ran down easily, he wound him up again to talk of his holiday.

'As for Tramonta,' said Clesant, taking the obstacle at a leap; he was sure that his uncle was working towards it; 'you know a man named Martin Whitby, I think.'

'Oh yes. I know him as Sir Hugh Borlase's son-in-law.'

'She was there too – his wife – and so was Lady Borlase.'

'Did you introduce yourself?'

'I never let them know I had heard of them.'

'You are the most absolute oyster,' cried Lance. 'You never let anyone know anything.'

'No harm in that,' said their uncle. 'To keep your mouth shut is one of the first rules of the game.'

'I've to say something I don't quite like,' continued Clesant, looking the Judge of Men between the eyes. 'I didn't go to Tramonta, on their account. I expect I'm all wrong, but I didn't care for them. They put me off.'

Mr Vullamy said nothing, but he was pleased.

'They meant to be decent, but they said things –'

'Lady Borlase?'

'No, the two Whitbies. They found out so much about me, that in the end, I set myself not to tell them. But they found out.'

'That you were my nephew?'

'No. Sir Adam. They recognized me in the old fresco – at least Whitby did. He saw it was an ancestor. I don't know how –' he went on, with a note of alarm. 'I've seen the photograph, and it's not the least like me. It was uncanny. I went to their hotel for an order to view the place, and Mrs Whitby asked me pointblank, and then said what nonsense ancestors were. I felt bound to tell you all this.'

Ignoring other points for a moment, Mr Vullamy said: 'Whitby understands art. That's interesting. What sort of resemblance?'

'I didn't wait. I was tired of the whole show. I didn't like his way of looking at things, nor he mine, and I'm afraid you may hear from him in London how I behaved, and that it was not gentlemanly, but from my point of view he was not gentlemanly either.'

'Nor from mine.'

Clesant tried to look indifferent, but he flushed because his judgement had been confirmed.

'You have found a very plausible person out. He's no friend of mine, and poor old Borlase feels the marriage a great mistake. He often talked to me.'

'Does he treat his wife badly?' said Clesant anxiously.

'My God, what a swine if he does!' muttered Lance.

But this could not be confirmed. Whitby treated his wife well, notoriously well. His sin was more subtle. 'I'll tell you about him if you like,' said Mr Vullamy, glancing at his watch. They would have preferred to be together, but they did not say so, indeed they scarcely knew it. To be talked to by Uncle Arthur was still the greatest of honours, and they lit their pipes.

'Whitby's the age,' he said rather sententiously, 'or what gets termed the age, though it's made of sterner stuff really, thank God.'

Lance, still upon the wrong track, murmured, 'How beastly.'

'I don't think Uncle Arthur means that.'

'Exactly,' said Mr Vullamy, again much pleased. 'Nothing as definite as beastliness, Clesant. I object to him really as an example of a type which is poisonous and spreading. Poisonous is too strong a word for it. Every word is too strong for it – that's the trouble. Mind, boys, you mustn't repeat this, for I know nothing against Whitby, who is an industrious and honest government servant. I wouldn't mind him if he didn't propagate the type and its ideas with such rapidity. He's against morality – but quietly, mind you, quietly; against religion, but quietly; against the Throne and all that we hold dear in the same way. Lance's Socialist on Bramley Down is open: we know where we are with him. The country's real danger is these crawling non-conformist intellectuals. A big war will clean them out – but till it comes –'

'Uncle Arthur,' said Lance, 'you'll get put in chokey. That'll be the end of you!'

'Not I! That isn't Whitby's line. He fights no one. His aim is to modify, till everything's slack and lukewarm. You agree, don't you?'

Clesant nodded.

'And when he has modified, then the real forces of evil – of which he has no conception – then they'll come in and take their turn. Oh, I'm wasting too many words on the fellow, but I've lately heard him hold forth at a debate against National Service. He argued in effect that if human nature was feebler, there'd be no more wars, and he wanted to enfeeble it. We were at the South London Institute, which was founded to produce better citizens, but the atmosphere has become socialist;[19] his sort of talk goes down there. I got up and said Mr Whitby was perfectly right: if human nature was feebler there would be no more wars: merely envy, hatred, malice and all uncharitableness.'

'Man must be a coward,' said Lance.

Mr Vullamy could not grant this either. Besides, he wanted to sketch Martin's character to his nephews. They would have to reckon with the type soon, and it was rather difficult: their young eyes, trained to see only light and darkness, might misunderstand it unassisted. Whitby was neither coward nor villain: he was a man without faith and infinitely dangerous. 'He won't fight,' he complained. 'It isn't that he can't or daren't, but he won't. He declares it unnecessary. Life will of course prove him wrong.'

'Yes indeed!' chorused the boys.

'To deny warfare is to deny good and evil. The question is extraordinarily simple when it's stated thus. As you know, I publish a good many books on military subjects – tactics, memoirs, and the rest of it – and also a certain amount of theology. The Radical press has chosen to make merry over this, but in all honesty I couldn't see the joke. I wish the rest of my life were as consistent.' He looked at his watch again. 'Before I go to your mother, I must give you a wigging, Clesant. You oughtn't to have allowed the Whitbies to put you off Tramonta, or influence your plans in any way. Because that's how they work – by putting people off. Of course I know how it was – they were inquisitive; but you shouldn't have.'

Clesant, who resented criticism, made no answer. Lance said, 'I should have done the same.'

'Then you too would have been wrong,' said Mr Vullamy lightly. 'Oh, it's only a little point, but in a sort of way – do you fellows follow me? – the Whitbies have defeated him.'

A rush of bad blood came over him, and he cursed his genealogical sisters. 'Come along, we're wasting Uncle

Arthur's time,' he said, rising almost rudely. 'No
been an awful fool.'

Their uncle watched them, smiling. Yes, C
shaping, and with the touch of Romance that p
edge on steel. He would make a fine younger son. He had scented the enemy by instinct, and his queasiness at following where they trod evinced the race in him. Lance, dear Lance, one had always known what he was – the joyous knight of the sabre who slashes and roars. But the rapier – may we not need that too in Armageddon? – and Clesant showed signs of proficiency.

He sought his sister, who like himself was fond of blood, and talked the boys over with her. He did not approve of talking but his visits to Monkswear were rare, and obliged him to get en rapport at once. 'I trust my boys,' she said calmly. 'They will never do anything that they will be ashamed to tell me.'

'The world's a big place,' he suggested: 'and it's a man's world. But they will never do anything that will shame your honour, Sophy. I guarantee that.'

Mrs March accepted the amendment.

As for the knights, they were on horseback and very happy. They conquered the steep ascent out of Monkswear, and half a dozen miles of road and moor. Life appeared to them as one long conquest, and they did not know that the hills and moors are in collusion with youth, and that their enemies were still their lovers. It was splendid to stand on the ridge of Bramley and see Shaddock from it, and to say, 'Now let's do Shaddock.' Presently Shaddock lay under their feet, done, and they saw the Cheviots and the sea. Another horseman was seen in the distance. It was necessary to outstrip him and then to race one another. It was necessary to gallop against the wind. Presently ıey heard the beautiful cry of otter hounds, and saw the hunt in the bend of the river below them. Down they went. They were lucky enough to come in for a kill, which seemed to them a pleasant spectacle. When the corpse had been torn to pieces, and they had helped to blood the rector's little boy, who had not been present at a kill before, they proceeded on their ride.

'I'm glad we happened on that,' said Clesant. 'I hate wasting a morning.'

Lance piously assented, and added, 'But there's always something.'

'No, but a kill...'

For the otter also had the honour to be in collusion with youth. Its death stamped the morning with peculiar splendour, and was recalled by Clesant in after years. On they rode, full of the gay chivalry that purified medieval warfare, and is said to purify war today, charming to everyone but their immediate victim, and only asking for new worlds to conquer. At the top of a hill they drew rein. Purple heather, black peat, blue sky. They liked the bright colouring and felt it to be a reward for taking proper exercise, as perhaps it was. Dismounting suddenly, Lance flung himself down full length. His horse looked at him with mild disapproval, as did his brother.

'Stiff?' he suggested; he was not always sure that Lance's actions were in good form.

'Oh no: I wanted to.'

'You'll get damp.'

'Thick bags.'

But Lance's actions were attractive. Clesant found that he wanted to sprawl in the heather too. He did not do so, for the yoke of the public school was still heavy on him. But he dismounted, tethered his horse, and sat in an easy and manly fashion on a small stone. It was midday. The air was silent except for rustling wind and the popping of shots from a shooting party across the valley. Everything was hot and splendid. Clesant felt for his cigarette-case, and brought out a letter with it, which he threw to his brother.

'What do you make of that?' he asked.

'Oh, the letter that's been waiting for you. Who's it from?'

'Read it aloud.'

'"Hotel Modena, Modena, Italy. August the 30th. Dear Mr March, I don't believe in apologies, yet mean to send you one. I am sincerely sorry for the trouble we gave you at Milan. We stumbled – I assure you by accident – into your private life, and didn't extricate ourselves with any skill. Please excuse us. No doubt I've worded my apology wrong, but I'm trying to put myself into your place, and to write a letter that I shouldn't mind receiving. I'm sending it to the Milan hotel, on the off-chance of it reaching you some day." – What's all this?'

'Read on.'

'"You may say, Why apologize at all? And why wait a week before doing it? My answer is this. I have just had a humiliating adventure, and been – I won't say a coward, for I don't think I am one, but been unequal to an emergency. In other words, if our positions had been reversed on Basle station, you would be dead. This has made me think of you, and wish to express my regrets for our clumsiness, and my sincere esteem. Should you ever care to follow the acquaintance up – I should – Gresham, Cambridge, will always find me. Yours truly, Martin Whitby." – Hullo!'

'What do you make of it?'

'Bit affected.'

'Is it?'

'I don't like "Please excuse us": it's effeminate. Bit long too. What happened at Basle?'

'I stopped him hurting his foot.'

'I wonder what he has funked. Oh, but look here, why didn't you show this to Uncle Arthur?'

'Ought I too?'

'Well, it was obvious.'

'Was it?'

' "Was it?" "Is it?" ' mimicked Lance. 'Can't we risk a definite statement on any point?'

'You see, it is like this,' said Clesant, slipping off his little stone. 'As I came over the moors this morning, I settled I'd tell Uncle Arthur why I'd failed to go if he asked me, and I knew he would, for he's wonderful at guessing where one has been a rotter. But I didn't settle about the letter, because I hadn't had it. When I had it, there was you playing the fool, and then breakfast, so I had to behave just as I felt at the time. When the time came, for some idiotic reason I didn't want to show it.'

'I think I should have.'

'Yes, I know. I was crooked. It is so infernal –' He frowned into the heather.

'You weren't crooked. But you are extraordinarily close.'

'They're the same thing. No, I don't mean that,' he added, recoiling from this abysmal truth. 'But I wish I wasn't close either. I seem always holding back something from somebody.'

'I've secrets I don't even tell you,' said Lance happily. 'It's natural now we're men.'

'I didn't like the Whitbies, and shall tear it up.' He did so, and looked thoughtfully at the pile of grey paper in his hand:

something remained to be said. 'But it's a grateful letter. It is that. And Uncle Arthur would only have laughed. I did nothing at Basle: I don't mean that, but Mr Whitby thinks no end of it, and says so at his own expense, and he'd do anything for me.'

CHAPTER SEVEN

If gratitude's the thing, Mr Vullamy should have been the person. The boys owed even more than they supposed to him; for the last ten years he had nourished them, body and soul. Their father had died in South Africa at the outbreak of the war[20] – a soldier's death, sudden, splendid, and expensive. Mr Vullamy had no children. He saw his opportunity, and determined to stage his sister and her family properly. Their life had been undignified hitherto; they had moved from house to house and been thrown with inferior people, and the boys had no real home to turn to in their holidays. His first step was to establish them at Monkswear.

The house was small but remarkable. It stood in a ravine, where a trout stream forced its way between two hills. The hill behind was heavily wooded, and down it wound the carriage's drive, with dangerous corners that made Mrs March's infrequent garden parties things of terror. The hill in front – over the stream – was a genuine precipice, with rocky facets and birch trees in the clefts, and below the stables and the little meadow the ravine closed in and the stream cried and pounded at its barriers as though strong enough to ruin the world. Seen from above the place suggested a lair, and Mr Vullamy entertained the notion willingly. He liked to think of its seclusion and of the brood that was growing up in it. Presently they would emerge from their cavern, shake themselves a bit – he was prepared for the shake – and steal upon the astonished prey. Non-conformist intellectuals would cry, 'What? do we still harbour such creatures in twentieth-century England?' and Mr Vullamy would retort, 'Yes; for while England is, they are.' He was a sensible man. He did not expect his nephews to save society or become prominent. But he did hope that through his efforts two more men of the right sort would be given to a world that needs them sorely. That would be his reward.

Nor was religion absent. The place suited his sister. The monks and their weir had gone, but there was a flavour of pre-Reformation times that consorted with her devotions. Since her husband's death she avoided society and seldom left her retreat, except to ministrate to the poor. They did not like her much, for she had south-country airs about her, but she went in spite of their rebuffs, the poor being part of her outlook, and was active in all attempts to organize them for their good. She loved her home – 'my hermitage' she called it plaintively – and ruled it with the efficiency of a Lady Abbess, making allowances, in a calm deliberate way, for the fervency of youth. For her own part she never regretted the sunlight and the wind: this shadowed garth was the best that this world could offer.

Mr Vullamy liked it too, but he could not have lived in it. His work and his inclinations took him among men. He had had an interesting career, first as school inspector, then as war correspondent, and now he was a partner in a respectable publishing firm. Incidentally he did much unpaid work, which brought him into contact with all sorts and conditions, and few men had glanced through more sections of society. But 'experience is a knack', and he brought out of life what he had taken into it: namely a profound belief in the gentlemanly middle classes. He championed them in print with extraordinary skill. 'Yes, yes,' he would say, 'we haven't poetry and art and we greatly admire those who have; far be it from us to pride ourselves. But –' And then he spoke of grit and honesty and latent idealism. ('It's damned latent', had been the comment of Dorothea Borlase.) All the middle classes needed was the discipline of war. It is true that they had had South Africa, but South Africa was too far away and against too small a foe. They needed Armageddon. His opinions were consistent: the belief of the coexistence of good and evil underlay his religious life as well as his political. Good would ultimately prevail, but the struggle is all that a man dare fix on. And pending the actual arrival of the enemy, he reserved his bitterest wrath for men like young Whitby, who prepared the way for they knew not what. He was a skilful if solid writer, and though his victims might laugh at him, or call him self-righteous and arrogant, it was felt that he scored in the long run, and that was all that he minded.

When his brother-in-law died, he also took in hand the boys' careers. Lance should have gone into the Army, but his sight was bad, so Clesant went instead; and had just passed out of Sandhurst without discredit. Lance was entering on his last year at Cambridge and then would read for the bar.[21] As for the girls, they would marry. They were both stupid, and in any case a woman's true career is motherhood. He was married himself, but had no children, and perhaps his continual exhortations to increase and multiply were due to this private disappointment. His wife, a hard chatty little woman, ran his house well, and seconded him in all his undertakings, but he turned gladly from her to his sister, a mother in Israel[22].

On this occasion he stopped a week. It was a real holiday. For one thing he had never to be on his guard. The household was both immature and friendly, and he could say what he liked without fear. His account of Socialism, for instance, was not as he would have given it at a London dinner table. It was simple, so that Olive could exclaim at the end of it, 'But Uncle Arthur, how *stupid* they must be.' He was a shrewd judge of a situation, and saw that the household was working just as he wished – his sister at the head, but free from vulgar worries, his nephews helpful and independent, his nieces helpful. He saw too that they were all fond of one another, and the only thing that he did not see was the warmth of the intimacy between the two young men. It was the fault of his outlook: he never realized how fond people may get of one another: judges of men don't. After the incident of the letter, the two trusted each other absolutely. They had shaken hands, as it were, behind their uncle's back.

During that happy September Clesant developed quickly. It was the luckiest thing that could have happened to him. His need all through life was an idol, and he found one for the moment in his own brother. As horrid little boys, they had got on as well as most horrid little boys, but afterwards they had been to different public schools, and met seldom. Consequently they had escaped all that makes brotherhood hard and banal, and came to each other with a touch of romance. Lance was the happiest influence. He was frank, called people fools but never sneered at them, and never thought that they were sneering at him, and he behaved to Clesant with the emotional ease that he had learned at Cambridge, treating him with open affection and consulting him in all he did. Clesant drew back at first; the son and heir wasn't quite dignified enough. Then he yielded, and a lump of ice melted that he might have carried about with him till death.

In future years he regretted that, having forged so great an instrument, they should have used it so feebly. They applied their friendship to trivialities. Were more ash trees to be cut? Should they take Olive or Joan to the match, or must it be both? Religion, the passions, and all serious subjects they ignored, because it is bad form to discuss them: an Englishman is assumed to be capable of understanding himself. At times Lance hinted at difficulties, but he always snubbed him, for if one begins one might never stop, and if Lance wanted to begin, he had Cambridge. One gathered there were men at Cambridge who could discuss a horse's head off.

The broadest hint – indeed it was a direct invitation – came just before he returned to Sandhurst. They had been over to a friend's moor – an impromptu affair, for the birds were wild and the beaters insufficient, but they had enjoyed it, and the ladies of the party had joined them with lunch, in spite of the rain. Tea at a farm, followed by a ten-mile drive together through the wet.

'I hate you going,' said Lance.

'You'll have to go yourself soon.'

After that they spoke little, oppressed by the shadow of change. Lance drove. Clesant had to soothe two spaniels, one mournful, the other affectionate, and to look after the guns. At first they kept to the road. Then, knowing the country well, they took a short cut by a track over fields, which saved them a mile, but there were gates, and each time he got down, the dogs got down too. But the last gate was opened for him: a girl who was passing on the highroad had heard their approach. The light from the lamp fell on her face peeping from a shawl. She was pretty. They thanked her, and drove on.

Presently Lance said, 'Do you go falling in love, Cles?'

Cautious at once he replied, 'How? Do you?'

'Yes. Off and on.'

Attempting the sort of chaff he had read in books, Clesant said: 'And who's the happy damsel? Ena Robins? One of the Brett girls.'

'You've not understood,' said his brother, whipping up the horse. 'I don't mean anything decent. It's getting a damned nuisance.'

Clesant felt miserably unhappy. He changed the conversation.

CHAPTER EIGHT

Martin's Italian holiday retreated quickly: holidays do as we grow older. After a month's work it seemed to have happened to another person. He had a good memory, and when there was time he could recall Tramonta, or scenes less pleasant, but the past like the future became less important to him, as he grew older and fixed his eyes on the piece of rope that was moving through his hand rather than on the coil he had built up and the tangle that he was diminishing. His work, his wife, his child, passed before him day after day, with a larger proportion of wife and child every seventh day, and subordinate to these, but equally constant, passed his amusements and hobbies and his friends. He touched them dexterously, not omitting the life of the spirit. But all that he did or felt vanished into an immense silence.

'I understand,' said Dorothea. 'Everything seems equally unimportant, but one slogs on.'

'Oh, you don't understand – not the very least. Everything is as important and of as varying importance as it ever was; at the time. But when it's over, it's over and with a thoroughness –! It falls into a chasm where no one will ever notice it. In my youth, especially in my more pious youth, when I did anything I thought with awe, "There I've done it!" and all the heavenly host began to comment on it and discuss it, while I went forward and did something else. This was inspiriting. One likes notice.'

'It is useless to brood on the past,' said his wife. 'One has to feed on the advancing hours, or take the consequences.'

'How can I help feeding on them? They advance down my very throat.'

'Indigestion. That's his trouble,' remarked Dorothea.

'Martin!' said a voice from the floor.

'Yes, my son?'

'Indi – Indi –'

'India what?'

'India-percha,' said Hugo, lost in the treacheries of language. They laughed and he laughed too, to show that he had lost himself for fun and not like some babies by mistake. 'India percha,' he repeated decidedly, adding, 'Please Martin will you sharpen me a cut pencil.'

'Why do you want a pencil when you're playing trains?'

'I want to draw a train with it.'

'But you draw a train with an engine, not with a pencil.'

Venetia frowned at him for muddling the child.

'The pencil draws the engine but the engine draws the train…'

'Then what does the train draw?'

'The pencil of course,' said Dorothea, detaching one from her chain and sticking it between the windows of a car. 'How dull some parents are.'

This had an immense success; the roar of locomotion filled the room.

'Now will you forget this as soon as you get to the office?' she asked, looking at her brother-in-law and smiling.

'Long before I get there. But the heavenly host may remember it.'

'How do you know they don't remember you?'

'I've an instinct they don't. If they do, I pity them, for all my thoughts and actions for the last month would bore them to tears. Dear me if one were isolated – how absolutely useless one would be.'

'Naturally,' said Venetia.

'But you and I and Dorothy in particular. We've crawled into little cells and there we're all right. But plunge us in the infinite or the sea, or one of those things, and we drown.'

Dorothea asked him why he did not call himself a pessimist and have done with it. He answered, quite simply: 'Because I retain this vision of Form. Put that in your pipe and smoke it. You and Nettie showed it to me years ago.'

'Form in civilization as it is, or as it will be?'

'As it will be. What I do in my little cell at the Treasury, helps to build it up.'

'And how if what you build up, I in my little cell at the Conservatoire or elsewhere pull down?'

'You don't. I've a vision you don't.'

'I agree with Dorothy,' said his wife. 'It's no good falling back on visions. What with militarism and what with snobbery, there are hundreds ready to pull down what we are building up. If one could only get *away* from people! If they would only *do* nothing one would have a chance. But take the Anti-Suffrage societies. As soon as they see we have collected funds, they send round to all the old ladies –'

While she was speaking, her husband glided from the room.

'He is too visionary,' she asserted.

'Yes, according to our notions. There never yet was a visionary in our family.' She went to the piano.

'Won't you clear?'

'No, I won't. I've a man coming with a new version. I must try these over.'

She began singing a folksong in scholarly fashion; she had collected half a dozen variants of it already:

> 'Oh he did whistle and she did sing –'

'Who are he and she?' asked Venetia, looking over her shoulder.

'Joseph and Mary. That's from Hereford. Now listen to this. Kent.

> 'Oh he did whistle and she did sing
> And all the bells of earth did ring
> For joy that Jesus Christ was born
> On Christmas day in the morning.

'Now for Wiltshire. The mode's Doric. "Oh he did –" '

'They sound to me very much alike,' said her sister, passing out with the breakfast things. Dorothea opened her notebook, the companion of many a country tramp. In it were her gleanings of English song. Her enthusiasm, cold and steady, had led her among queer places and rough men. There were entries in it such as 'Mr Lodge, Imber in the Down. Only when drunk.' 'Mrs Tarr, Blandford Workhouse.' Some of the verses were unprintable. All that was beautiful and pure – and there was much – would be sifted out of the chaff, and resown. In other words, the songs could be taught back in schools to the grandchildren of those who had known them instinctively. This was Miss Borlase's work, and she meant to give up her life to it. For the next four years she would collect: there would be less to collect each year, partly because the field was being worked by her colleagues, partly because the old people were dying out. When the four years were up, she would teach, or press the claims of teaching. At present folksong and Morris were fashionable – London ladies liked them at At Homes – but in four years she expected the ebb, and must work through it, and save the moment from death or vulgarity.

At ten the doorbell rang. 'Here he is,' she called to her sister, who was finishing her duties in the kitchen. 'I'll let him in. Pray that he's not full of fleas.' Hugo took her hand and they ran down the passage, expecting to find an aged window-cleaner from Pimlico who had sung the sun up over the Wrekin in his youth. Ah no! It was a gentleman. Dorothea's face fell. He wanted Mr Whitby.

'He's at the office. – Venetia! Will Martin be in to lunch?'

'Yes,' called her sister, and then appeared. 'Oh, how do you do!' she said. 'I remember your face abroad. What is it?'

'Couldn't I see him now?'

'Not very well. Is it important?'

'Yes;' he was holding a telegram.

'Aunt Dolly, why doesn't he sing?' asked Hugo.

'Would you like to telephone to him at the Treasury?'

'I should have preferred to talk. I know that he's a Fellow of Gresham, and he might have been able to explain this. It's from a brother of mine.' He held it out. They read: 'Sent down this afternoon. Stick to me. Lance.'

Venetia folded it up and returned it. 'I don't think my husband could help you,' she said. 'He's not in residence, and has nothing to do with the discipline.'

'There's been some mistake, which I want to put right as soon as possible. Mr Whitby wrote to me saying he would help me at any time.'

'I didn't know. I daresay.'

'What's your brother's name?' asked Dorothea.

'March.'

'Why, I've danced with him. Of course it's a mistake.'

'I say, what am I to do?' he cried, turning to her. 'I had it this morning at Sandhurst. I want to put it right at once.'

She went to the telephone. 'I'll ring up my father. That'll be the simplest. It's no good wasting time over Martin.' While she was waiting for the trunk call she said, 'I believe he's pulling your leg.'

'But you know him quite well!' exclaimed Clesant. 'But then you mustn't ring up your father.'

'Oh, I don't the least mind pulling his. Does him good. I liked your brother, and I liked the way he dances.'

'He's not thought much of, too clumsy,' said the other, smiling.

'That's what people would say, because they like a man who dances from the outside. I like one who dances from the inside. It's no good the feet being in the right place when the heart's in the wrong one. He dances as men danced before they were cooped into ballrooms and joy disappeared.'

'I'll tell him what you say.'

'I told him myself... Can you keep any secrets from him? I couldn't.'

Clesant took to her at once: though unlike anyone he had met, she did not repel him. 'Why does this kid keep asking me to sing?' he inquired, indicating Hugo.

'Sing him something, and see if he asks you again.'

He laid his hand on the child's head and waggled it.

'No, I am expecting an aged man and he thinks you are he. I collect folksongs.'

'Why do you do that?'

'Because they are beautiful. – There's your call –. I'll send you and your brother tickets for my next recital if you'll come.' She took up the receiver and he heard her say: 'Are you the Lodge, Gresham?... Miss Borlase... I want to speak to the Master.' Then a pause. 'Hullo papa... I want to know whether a man named March has been sent down... Oh?... Why?... Well, his brother's here. Will you tell him? – Here, you have a try,' she cried, handing it to Clesant. 'My father won't tell me.'

'Is it true?'

'Apparently.'

They looked at each other without flinching.

It was the first time he had used a telephone, and all his life it was to feel like eavesdropping into Hell. Supposing that he must raise his voice if it was to reach Cambridge he said lustily, 'I want to know if this is true about my brother?'

Inside his own head an aged pulchinello[23] replied: 'You need not shout so. It is perfectly unnecessary.' Buzzing continued, in the midst of which lay the corpses of words.

'Speak up, speak up,' said Clesant, unable to realize that he was talking to a living man and a D.C.L.[24]

'Extraordinary meeting of the Disciplinary Board,' said pulchinello.

'What's the charge against him?'

He heard, '– Proctors – found him last night – disrepute.'

'Oh indeed,' said Clesant, putting his free hand on his hip and raising his voice again. 'It's all very well to say that down a tube to me, but I'd like you to repeat it to my face. My brother couldn't act dishonourably. I don't know who started your lie, but it is a lie, and I call out the man who started it. Who do you have for proctors? Why don't you employ gentlemen?…' He lowered the receiver and Hell vanished. He was back in a London flat with two women and a pretty little child. He was filled with horror in case he had said anything unfit for them to hear, and in his dazed state thought that they had heard pulchinello too. 'What am I to do with this?' he said feebly.

'Put it back on the rest if you've done with it,' Dorothea replied.

'He looks very hot,' said Hugo.

'Mr March, are you going to Cambridge?'

'Yes, at once.'

'Well, take my brother-in-law with you. He can manage it – it's Saturday.'

'He can be asked,' said Venetia, who had hoped to take him to an At Home.

Dorothea was again at the telephone, and in a minute had made all the arrangements. 'It must be put right now,' she told them. 'We can't have him leaving Cambridge in disgrace, even if he's called back in an hour. Trust Martin. Tell him everything. He's very *very* good at sifting a misunderstanding. And remember me to your brother.'

Clesant was too much moved to speak. He had never met with such sympathy from a woman, and in recognition of it he performed the first beautiful action of his life. He laid his hand on Hugo's head, and his lips on his hand. When he had gone Dorothea cried: 'How much did papa hear of that last speech? I expect he switched off at once, but oh that he had heard every word of it.'

'What was it all about? I haven't yet understood, except that someone has not behaved like a gentleman.'

'Mother will tell us. Let's ring up her.'

And presently Lady Borlase's voice came, dehumanized but audible. March and two other men were to be sent down: it was a dreadful thing for the college.

'More dreadful for the college than for the men,' commented Dorothea. 'I wonder how long Cambridge will pretend she holds the keys of Hell and Heaven. Imagine such an escapade being treated seriously at a Foreign University! Imagine Paris or Bonn or Bologna pompously ruining three boys for life! They'd be boycotted, and so will Cambridge be when England regains her senses.'

'Discipline must be maintained,' said her sister.

'Oh yes, you've married a don.'

'Most certainly we agree on this point.'

'Yes, but Martin has fairness – an almost superhuman fairness – and he'll see that the Marches have a proper run for their money. If anyone can hold papa and the whole University up, he will.'

'Dorothy, why have you taken so much trouble over this?'

'Because I fell in love with the undergraduate one during a dance.'

The news was received calmly. Dorothea always was saying that she fell in love with men. She only meant that Lance was not disagreeable to her, and could have said the same about Clesant. By such overstatements the young lady made up for the thousands of young ladies who have pretended not to fall in love until they are loved. As a girl, Venetia had joined with her. But Venetia was a matron now, and only risqué when duty called her.

While they were talking, the window-cleaner called. He was a disappointment, knew no folksong, but would sing a ballad about his mother and glory, and was difficult to get rid of. Dorothea then played Pergolesi, to drive all interruption from her ears.

CHAPTER NINE

They met at the station, and on Martin's side with friendliness. It was always pleasant to be a success, and the letter, which he regretted as soon as posted, had hit the mark after all. It was strange that he should care for the approval of an insignificant youth, but then it is strange that one should care for anyone's approval, and behind young March lay something big that he was curious to unveil. He was anxious to stand well with him and help him.

He took a serious view of the situation. Whatever the faults of his father-in-law, hastiness was not among them, so that Lance was either guilty or would find it impossible to prove his innocence. Martin himself was a disciplinarian. He denied that any institution could be run on Dorothea's lines. But, as she said, he was also superhumanly fair. He sought for the path of least disaster.

Clesant wired to his brother that he was coming up to clear him. Martin did not see the wire, but he gathered its sense from conversation. He tried to put some shading into the boy's black-and-white mind, but found it difficult.

'You mustn't be too rough on anyone,' he hazarded. 'Mistakes will happen.'

'It's no mistake, Mr Whitby. It's a conspiracy.'

'Not likely,' said Martin, 'There are very few plots in these days. I am in the Civil Service, supposed a hotbed of intrigue, and I come across many misunderstandings, but very few plots. You can't suggest that the University authorities have a down on your brother?'

'I don't know why not. A master had a down on him at school.'

'I can only go by myself, but I've never hated anyone, and as far as I know no one has ever hated me.' Feeling that he had now given the other as much milk-and-water as he could swallow, he took up the *Saturday Westminster* – that sea-green incorruptible![25] – occasionally stealing a glance over its pages. March was smoking, his eyes very blue. He could hate and imagine himself hated, and Martin puzzled over the attractiveness of such a mind. One disapproved of it and had honestly no temptation to copy, and yet desired the owner as a friend. He would be a feather in one's cap – most curious! He might help one to tighten up the will.

Though he laughed at Cambridge, Martin enjoyed a weekend there, and felt absurdly important when their hansom drew up at the side-gate of Gresham, and the porter ran out of his hot stone hole, touching his hat. After all, he was a Fellow, and son-in-law to the Master. He was not without authority in the place. Having sent his suitcase to the Lodge, he cut over the wet grass to Lance's rooms – of course it was raining. There was a light in the window.

'I won't come in,' he said, suddenly nervous.

'I'd like you to, we've nothing to hide.'

'Oh, then I'll come.'

Clesant went in, without knocking; Mr Vullamy reading, his hand over his eyes, gave him the first hint of disaster. 'Oh, what are you here for?' he cried.

'I had a wire like yourself. There's nothing to be done.'

'Uncle Arthur, have you found out who set it about?'

'My dear boy, he's guilty. Didn't you realize?'

Clesant walked to the window.

'Who's that you've brought with you? Oh, Mr Whitby: how do you do. But may I ask what you are here for?'

'To be of any use I could… I'm stopping at the Lodge this evening.'

'I have already been to the Lodge. Sir Hugh's an old friend of mine, and would have been lenient to my nephew if possible. But it is impossible. He has disgraced the college and himself. He has disgraced me and his brother there. At present he is packing, and when he's finished I take him away. I can't blame the authorities. They have behaved with propriety throughout.'

Martin disliked this speech. It was dignified, but nothing else.

'Where am I to take him to?' he continued. 'You can assist me on that point. Am I to send him home to his mother? Am I to admit him to my own house, where my wife is entertaining her friends? Can I trust him alone?'

'If this is genuine difficulty and not merely a way of expressing your disapproval,' said Martin; 'if it is a genuine difficulty, I can help you. There is room for him at my London flat. My wife also is entertaining but she can receive him and not vex him with questions. I can send her a note. He can remain there till you have arranged something.'

'Oh, how very kind, but we have the habit here of taking our disasters seriously. Lance has got to suffer.'

'I am right then in thinking that your difficulty might not be genuine.'

'Like your kind offer, perhaps.'

But why were they fighting? Martin checked himself. It was ridiculous. He murmured, 'No, I meant what I said,' and was silent. Mr Vullamy turned to his nephew.

'As you're in Cambridge, you must call at the Lodge and apologize to Sir Hugh for what you said to him down the telephone.

No answer.

'I have explained to him. He understands, and you will find him lenient.'

'If he understands, why need your nephew call?' burst from Martin.

'Because Sir Hugh, like myself, is old-fashioned and expects courtesy from the younger generation.'

'He has scored again,' thought Martin. 'What did I do it for?' And still the desire for battle remained. Something in the room provoked it. He wanted – not to win: nothing so commonplace as that; but to slash with all the force of soul and body against what he considered wrong: against unkindness; Mr Vullamy was fundamentally unkind, and loved neither of his nephews at bottom – he was only proud of them.

'Mr Whitby, if I may say so you had better leave us now.'

'He asked me to come,' he replied, pointing to Clesant, who had never moved or spoken.

'It is not his room.'

'I know. It is his brother's, at whose request I shall leave it, and at whose only.'

'Lance!' cried Mr Vullamy, tapping at the bedroom door. Lance came out, and with him their skirmish ended, for Clesant was across the room crying: 'Is it true? Is it true?'

'Don't make a scene,' said his uncle.

Lance nodded his head. 'Who's that?' he said hopelessly, looking at Martin.

'But you wired I was to stick to you.'

'I know, Cles.'

'But what did you mean?'

'Oh, never mind now.'

'If it's true, how can I?'

'Yes, it is true.'

'Have you thought of mother at all?' asked Clesant.

'Finish your packing first, Lance. Ask that gentleman if he will kindly leave your room. He is a hindrance.'

Again he looked at Martin and said: 'I don't know him. I don't mind anything. Where am I to go?'

His brother said: 'No one will have you, Uncle Arthur says. I won't. Don't come near me.'

'I'm sorry,' said Lance, speaking with increasing difficulty, like a man under the sea.

'Old Armstrong was sorry, but you sacked him, Lance, that's what I can't get over – you've been a hypocrite. That's what mother won't forgive you. I've been thinking – in the window – you've deceived me. I can't trust anyone again. I look up to you, and you do this – take to filth and go with women. I've your letter and one Olive sent on to me – both written this week – and you talk about rowing and your work, and make jokes. Then you expect to come home.' His voice grew firmer. 'Never. Never if I have a word. You have disgraced us. We can never lift our heads again.'

He murmured something.

'That's babyish. You're "sorry" because you're found out. Men are never sorry. You know that as well as I do. You'll go from bad to worse. You'll do it again.' Then he exploded: 'Oh, you swine – you lout with a gentleman's face – get away from us to your own sort and do it again. Go to Hell. I was to stick to you, was I, you wallowing filthy swine? I was your sort, and follow you into filth. I want – I curse you.'

Again he murmured.

'I curse you in the name of our mother.'

'Steady on,' said Mr Vullamy.

'Steady on indeed,' said Martin.

Lance had gone into his room by this time, closing the door after him. Clesant returned to the window. The other two glanced at each other nervously, their little tiff quite forgotten. Both were shocked, Mr Vullamy most. Martin, who was younger, could reflect that Clesant was very young, and that no mature man would have made such a terrible speech. Here was the violence of inexperience, the cruelty of one who has never been tempted himself. He hadn't felt, he didn't know. In time, he would repent bitterly, and Lance, clearly a fine nature, would forgive him and love him better than before.

In the midst of his reflections, he heard a noise, not unlike the popping of a paper bag. He should have taken no notice, but Mr Vullamy rushed into the bedroom with a cry. The boy had shot himself.

NOTES

1. The more usual term is a 'Wykehamist', someone who has attended Winchester College.
2. French politician and writer Jean Jaurès (1859–1914) was the founder of the socialist paper *l'Humanitè*.
3. The Nottingham and Derby Railway was a fictitious railway, presumably invented by Forster for the purposes of this debate. It makes a further appearance in *Howards End*, where Margaret Schlegel is described as having invested in it.
4. David Lloyd George (1863–1945) was Chancellor of the Exchequer from 1908 to 1915, and Prime Minister from 1916 to 1922. In 1911, the time Forster commenced work on *Arctic Summer*, he was working on the controversial National Insurance Bill to provide insurance for the working class against unemployment and sickness.
5. Tramonta is a fictitious place, believed to be based on Malpaga, near Bergamo in northern Italy. Forster perhaps derived the name from *tramontana*, the north wind.
6. A fictitious artist.
7. Vincenzo Bellini (1801–35) was an Italian composer whose works proved inspirational to the Italian Risorgimento; Giuseppe Mazzini (1805–72), an Italian nationalist and patriot, was one of the heroes of the Risorgimento.
8. The Re Galantuomo (the Upright King) is Victor Emmanuel II (1820–78), the first king of unified Italy (1861–78).
9. My God!
10. Estate manager.
11. Peasants.
12. Monsalvat has echoes of both Montsalvat, the legendary mountain said to be found guarding the Castle of the Holy Grail, and Montserrat, the pinaccled mountain in northern Spain, said to have been shattered when Christ was crucified; Asgard is the fortress of the northern gods that can be reached only by way of the rainbow bridge.
13. The 1571 Battle of Lepanto was the first major defeat of the Ottomans by the Christians and halted the advance of the Ottoman Empire through the Mediterranean.
14. Mendelism is the system of heredity as formulated from the research of Gregor Mendel (1822–84).
15. In his 1951 revisions, Forster began standardising Venetia's sister's name to Dorothea, but there are some instances where Dorothy remains.
16. Following his reading of the previous five chapters at the Aldeburgh Festival in 1951, Forster went on to say that he considered the remainder of the work to be of a lesser quality. He also identified a number of problems with the text, namely: that the character of March ought to be allowed to 'come and go, and not be too documented'

whereas Chapter Six describes him in his family circle; that it was not immediately obvious how he could again link the lives of March and Whitby (although he then went on to describe a possible solution which is more or less the basis of the plot of Chapters Six to Nine); and, more importantly, that he had never decided how to complete the book: 'I had not settled what was going to happen, and that is why the novel remains a fragment. The novelist should I think always settle when he starts what is going to happen, what his major event is to be... I cannot tell you what happened in *Arctic Summer*, and even the First Great War, which broke out the next year, did not tell me. In a sense I see more clearly today, for I have lived on to an age where not only March can't get what he wants but Martin can't get it either. The novel might have ended with the two as companions in defeat. But such an ending doesn't interest me.' Forster therefore did not revise the remainder of *Arctic Summer* and the manuscript was left incomplete.

17. According to the myth, the priest Laocoön warned the Trojans about the wooden horse; the gods sent two vast serpents which tore Laocoön and his two sons apart.

18. Writer and clergyman Charles Kingsley (1819–75) and John Henry Newman (1801–90) exchanged a series of pamphlets following Kingsley's controversial comments on Catholics. These culminated in the publication of Newman's *Apologia pro vita sua* (1864).

19. The South London Institute appears to have had links with the British Secular Movement.

20. The Boer War (1899–1902), claimed the lives of thousands of British soldiers; Boer casualties were considerably higher.

21. This is, of course, an inconsistency on Forster's part, as earlier in the text (p. 51) Lance says he is 'to be a publisher'.

22. 'A mother in Israel' refers to the besieged city of Abel Beth Maacah, where the 'troublemaker' Sheba had taken refuge. The city was saved when Sheba's head was presented to Joab (II Samuel 20: 19).

23. Pulchinello was the clown character in *commedia dell'arte*, and a very early version of 'Punch' in 'Punch and Judy' shows.

24. The degree of Doctor of Civil Law is awarded by Oxford University to graduates of the university for published work, and also as an honorary degree.

25. The *Saturday Westminster* was a spin-off from the *Westminster Gazette*, a highly regarded liberal newspaper; a tinge of green can be identified on some of its pages. The term 'the seagreen Incorruptible' was first used by Thomas Carlyle (1795–1881) to describe Robespierre in his *History of the French Revolution* (1837).

BIOGRAPHICAL NOTE

Edward Morgan Forster was born in London in 1879 to Edward Forster, an architect, and Alice Whichelo. He was educated at Tonbridge School and then went on to King's College, Cambridge, where he met many members of the future Bloomsbury Group. He retained a lifelong association with King's College and was elected to an Honorary Fellowship in 1946.

On leaving Cambridge in 1901, Forster travelled through Europe for a year; his experiences and observations of his fellow-tourists providing material for his early novels. Once back in England, he began writing for the newly launched *Independent Review*, and in 1905 he completed his first novel, *Where Angels Fear to Tread*. This was followed by *The Longest Journey* (1907), *A Room with a View* (1908), and *Howards End* (1910). By now he was firmly established as a writer of considerable importance.

In 1912, he visited India and the ensuing *A Passage to India* (1924) was awarded the Prix Femina Vie Heureuse and the James Tait Black Memorial Prize. This was to be his last novel; *Maurice*, which was written in 1913, was not published until after his death, in 1971. Instead, Forster devoted his life to a range of literary activities, notably his strong stance against censorship. His famous work of literary criticism *Aspects of the Novel* appeared in 1927, and by this time he was regularly lecturing at Cambridge. He also penned a collection of essays, a biography, and, with Eric Crozier, the libretto for Benjamin Britten's *Billy Budd* (1951). Upon his death in 1970, *The Times* hailed him as among 'the most esteemed English novelists of his time'.

HESPERUS PRESS – 100 PAGES

Hesperus Press, as suggested by the Latin motto, is committed to bringing near what is far – far both in space and time. Works written by the greatest authors, and unjustly neglected or simply little known in the English-speaking world, are made accessible through new translations and a completely fresh editorial approach. Through these short classic works, each around 100 pages in length, the reader will be introduced to the greatest writers from all times and all cultures.

For more information on Hesperus Press, please visit our website: **www.hesperuspress.com**

ET REMOTISSIMA PROPE

SELECTED TITLES FROM HESPERUS PRESS

Author	*Title*	*Foreword writer*
Pietro Aretino	*The School of Whoredom*	Paul Bailey
Jane Austen	*Love and Friendship*	Fay Weldon
Honoré de Balzac	*Colonel Chabert*	A.N. Wilson
Charles Baudelaire	*On Wine and Hashish*	Margaret Drabble
Giovanni Boccaccio	*Life of Dante*	A.N. Wilson
Charlotte Brontë	*The Green Dwarf*	Libby Purves
Mikhail Bulgakov	*The Fatal Eggs*	Doris Lessing
Giacomo Casanova	*The Duel*	Tim Parks
Miguel de Cervantes	*The Dialogue of the Dogs*	
Anton Chekhov	*The Story of a Nobody*	Louis de Bernières
Wilkie Collins	*Who Killed Zebedee?*	Martin Jarvis
Arthur Conan Doyle	*The Tragedy of the Korosko*	Tony Robinson
William Congreve	*Incognita*	Peter Ackroyd
Joseph Conrad	*Heart of Darkness*	A.N. Wilson
Gabriele D'Annunzio	*The Book of the Virgins*	Tim Parks
Dante Alighieri	*New Life*	Louis de Bernières
Daniel Defoe	*The King of Pirates*	Peter Ackroyd
Marquis de Sade	*Incest*	Janet Street-Porter
Charles Dickens	*The Haunted House*	Peter Ackroyd
Fyodor Dostoevsky	*Poor People*	Charlotte Hobson
Joseph von Eichendorff	*Life of a Good-for-nothing*	
George Eliot	*Amos Barton*	Matthew Sweet
F. Scott Fitzgerald	*The Rich Boy*	John Updike
Gustave Flaubert	*Memoirs of a Madman*	Germaine Greer
Ugo Foscolo	*Last Letters of Jacopo Ortis*	Valerio Massimo Manfredi
Elizabeth Gaskell	*Lois the Witch*	Jenny Uglow
Théophile Gautier	*The Jinx*	Gilbert Adair

André Gide	*Theseus*	
Nikolai Gogol	*The Squabble*	Patrick McCabe
Thomas Hardy	*Fellow-Townsmen*	Emma Tennant
Nathaniel Hawthorne	*Rappaccini's Daughter*	Simon Schama
E.T.A. Hoffmann	*Mademoiselle de Scudéri*	Gilbert Adair
Victor Hugo	*The Last Day of a Condemned Man*	Libby Purves
Joris-Karl Huysmans	*With the Flow*	Simon Callow
Henry James	*In the Cage*	Libby Purves
Franz Kafka	*Metamorphosis*	Martin Jarvis
Heinrich von Kleist	*The Marquise of O–*	Andrew Miller
D.H. Lawrence	*The Fox*	Doris Lessing
Leonardo da Vinci	*Prophecies*	Eraldo Affinati
Giacomo Leopardi	*Thoughts*	Edoardo Albinati
Nikolai Leskov	*Lady Macbeth of Mtsensk*	Gilbert Adair
Niccolò Machiavelli	*Life of Castruccio Castracani*	Richard Overy
Katherine Mansfield	*In a German Pension*	Linda Grant
Guy de Maupassant	*Butterball*	Germaine Greer
Herman Melville	*The Enchanted Isles*	Margaret Drabble
Francis Petrarch	*My Secret Book*	Germaine Greer
Luigi Pirandello	*Loveless Love*	
Edgar Allan Poe	*Eureka*	Sir Patrick Moore
Alexander Pope	*Scriblerus*	Peter Ackroyd
Alexander Pushkin	*Dubrovsky*	Patrick Neate
François Rabelais	*Gargantua*	Paul Bailey
François Rabelais	*Pantagruel*	Paul Bailey
Friedrich von Schiller	*The Ghost-seer*	Martin Jarvis
Percy Bysshe Shelley	*Zastrozzi*	Germaine Greer
Stendhal	*Memoirs of an Egotist*	Doris Lessing
Robert Louis Stevenson	*Dr Jekyll and Mr Hyde*	Helen Dunmore

Theodor Storm	*The Lake of the Bees*	Alan Sillitoe
Italo Svevo	*A Perfect Hoax*	Tim Parks
W.M. Thackeray	*Rebecca and Rowena*	Matthew Sweet
Leo Tolstoy	*Hadji Murat*	Colm Tóibín
Ivan Turgenev	*Faust*	Simon Callow
Mark Twain	*The Diary of Adam and Eve*	John Updike
Giovanni Verga	*Life in the Country*	Paul Bailey
Jules Verne	*A Fantasy of Dr Ox*	Gilbert Adair
Edith Wharton	*The Touchstone*	Salley Vickers
Oscar Wilde	*The Portrait of Mr W.H.*	Peter Ackroyd
Virginia Woolf	*Carlyle's House and Other Sketches*	Doris Lessing
Virginia Woolf	*Monday or Tuesday*	Scarlett Thomas
Emile Zola	*For a Night of Love*	A.N. Wilson